Thomas

The Five Shifter Rules

Always put your mate before yourself.

Respect another shifter's mate.

Do nothing to expose the existence of shifters.

Do no unnecessary harm to shifters or humans.

Respect all nonhumans.

V.A. Dold

Table of Contents

THOMAS: Le Beau Series

ISBN–13: 978-0990523543
ISBN–10: 0990523543

Print edition April 2015

V.A. Dold

This is Dedicated

To all of my readers and fans of the Le Beau Series, I appreciate you more than I can say.

Thank you to my friends and family who cheered me on and gave me the energy to keep writing when I was running low on sleep.

A special thank you to all the Bayou Babes who support me every day.

Thank you, Denise Greathouse Griffin, Karen Hall, & Christa Reed for your input and ideas for the proposal dinner.

BJ Gaskill, Mary Pavek, and Carolyn: you rock!

...Enjoy the adventure!

Thomas

Le Beau Series
Book 4

By

V.A. Dold

V.A. Dold

Prologue– The Plan

Only the birds singing and the leaves ruffling in the breeze shared Emma's solitude. Reverently, she knelt before the dais constructed for John's conversion. As part of its preparation, she had taken her daily meditation time at its base.

Closing her eyes and lifting her hands in supplication, she began to pray. "Mother Luperca, I ask that you bless this holy site and give it your approval."

As she knelt quietly, a soft voice greeted her, "Beloved daughter, I give this site my approval. All is prepared for my newest son, John, to join my family."

"May I also inquire about my unmated sons?"

"You ask about your sons, but that is not what I feel in your heart. Your true concern is for Thomas, and the plan I have for him."

"If it pleases you, may I be honored with the knowledge of your plan?"

"Thomas is destined to be Julia's mate."

"How may I be of assistance in bringing this mating to fruition?"

V.A. Dold

"Julia will attend the gathering. Ensure that they meet."

"Thank you, Mother. How may I be of further service?"

"Your daily worship pleases me well, child. You do enough. Blessed be."

"Blessed be, Mother."

Emma completed her prayers and final preparations, excited to tell Isaac her news.

*****

Isaac sat in his office responding to emails from the other pack patriarchs. The gathering was shaping up to be a complete success with every family in the region attending.

"Isaac! Isaac, where are you, cher?" Emma called through the house.

"In here, mon amour."

"I can't believe it!" Emma perched in the chair opposite him. "The Goddess has given me the next mate."

"Who?" he asked excitedly. "Lucas? Marcus?"

Emma leaned toward him and whispered her incredible secret. "Thomas."

"No! How?"

"Julia." Emma clapped excitedly. "She's his mate."

"I never saw that coming." Isaac laughed.

"That's why he isn't being converted with John."

Isaac nodded. "He'll be converted by Julia during the ritual."

"The Goddess told me Julia will attend the gathering, and our job is to ensure they meet."

THOMAS: Le Beau Series

"All right," Isaac grinned, "that should be easy enough. I'll keep tabs on Thomas, and you watch Julia. If they don't meet on their own, one of us will make sure they are introduced."

Several days later

The new moon had arrived. Anna was lighting candles while Emma busily prepared the dais.

The ritual was surprisingly easy. As the women knelt before the icon of Luperca, John laid face up on the dais.

Emma and Anna quietly prayed, requesting the wolf goddess to join them and grant John, his wolf soul.

The limbs on the tree above them gently swayed in a breeze that hadn't been there a moment ago. Her soft voice was heard before she shimmered into form.

"Rise, my beloved daughters, and await my new son at home."

Anna glanced at Emma, alarm evident in her eyes.

"It'll be fine," Emma whispered encouragingly. "Come, he'll join us shortly."

Once they were alone, the goddess focused on John. "John James, what do you ask of me?"

"I ask for conversion. I ask for the gift of a wolf's soul, and I humbly ask to join your family," he recited.

"Close your eyes."

The wind swirled around John and then suddenly stilled. Something filled his chest, creating a tightness that eased after a moment.

"You request is granted."

One instant he was human and the next a dark-colored wolf lay on the dais.

"Your chosen father, Cade Le Beau, awaits you beyond those trees. Go, learn the way of my children."

Chapter 1

"Hello?" Julia Le Beau yawned into the phone.

Her alarm never had the chance to go off, because her mother, Lucinda, beat it by a good thirty minutes. She was convinced the woman could hear her biological clock ticking, which was ridiculous since she had another six hundred years for children. No matter what Julia said, it didn't seem to penetrate her mother's ears, so, here she was, having the same conversation again.

"Julia, are you still in bed? Did you forget I'm bringing another family to your house this morning?"

"I thought I told you not to bring them. I'm finished with your parades, Mother."

"For Goddess sake, get showered immediately. We'll be at your door in one hour."

"I'm not going to answer the door, so don't bother."

Her mother ignored her as usual and exactly one hour later was at her door.

Julia hung her head in frustration. She lost count years ago how many men her mother brought for the 'sniff' test. Each time it was the same: no mate. Like the Little Engine That Could©, Lucinda refused to give up.

The last time Julia locked the door and ignored her mother's knocking, it resulted in a very ugly scene. Lucinda in the throws of an angry tirade was not a pretty sight. Her face turned a mottled shade of red, and she broke the door down, dragging the shocked men in behind her.

Since that day, she'd grudgingly opened the door. If not for her house's sake, then for the sake of the men, she could at least spare them the humiliation of the tantrum sure to happen.

Two hours later, Julia's stomach churned. She loathed the questions that came after each 'visit'. Couldn't her mother forget to ask, just once?

"Well?" her mother asked impatiently from the doorway.

"Nothing," Julia mumbled, not bothering to look up from the romance novel she was reading. "I had no attraction. No, scent. No, telepathy." She didn't even bother to say she was sorry this time because she wasn't.

Lucinda snarled in frustration as she came fully into the room.

"I met all the men you just paraded through my house and had none of the mating signs. I don't know what more you expect from me." She sighed wearily.

"I expect you to accept one."

Julia's chin fell to her chest as a heavy sigh escaped. "You know as well as I do, it doesn't work that way."

"I'm sure if you made the extra effort to at least date them, something would shake loose. How hard can it be? Just look at Cade and that human, Anna, they met in a bar in the French Quarter of all places. Not to mention, Simon and his mate Rose, yet another human to dilute the royal gene pool. Rose showed up at Cade's house after she lost her job in Denver, and now the family is stuck with her. And I heard a rumor that Stefan has found his mate, and you guessed it, a human. He bought her at the auction Simon had a couple months ago. I can't believe Isaac can still hold his head up in public with his sons mating lowlife humans. My daughters will mate pureblood shifters and maintain the integrity of the bloodline."

Julia wanted to scream. A mating didn't just 'shake loose', and there was nothing wrong with humans. Heck, most mates were human. There was no reasoning with her mother anymore. That ability had left the building along with Elvis years ago. She wasn't sure if the animal part of her mother was taking over and acting erratic or if the human side was slipping into insanity.

Her mother leaned forward forcing Julia to sit back. "For years, you have rejected the males I bring to you. It's time you made a—"

"Mother, I know you want your children mated, but no matter how badly you want it, you can't force it."

"Just watch me," Lucinda spat. "We are in line to gain the throne. The lineage must be continued and ready at all times."

It was true the family needed to continue, but mates and children came into a shifter's life when the Goddess deemed it was the right time. The last thing you wanted to do was push the Goddess or try to circumvent her plan. Thinking that way was suicide.

Lucinda turned on her heel toward the door and then paused. "There will be a group of available males here Friday. This pack is out of Arizona. Pray one of them is acceptable to you."

Once Lucinda was in her boat and headed out of her private bay, Julia finally breathed easy again. Krystal would be home in a few hours and available to talk. They needed a plan; somehow they needed to find a way to approach Father about Mother's behavior. The problem was her father, Charles, was completely blind to her mother's oddities.

Julia turned the page of her book and settled deeper into her favorite easy chair; there was nothing she could do until Krystal got home. Tonight she would suggest again they bring Logan and Quintin into the conversation. It was about time the boys knew what was going on behind the family's back. Thinking it through, she shook her head. She wouldn't bother the twins, Rémi, and René, just yet. They were too young to be drawn into this.

Once Lucinda got a notion in her head, she had a tendency to twist it until it fit her needs and desires. After that, she could never be swayed.

And her mother's drive to force both Krystal and Julia to find mates had reached critical mass.

"What are we going to do?" Julia whispered to herself.

Two weeks later

Morning was Julia's favorite time of day. The bar wasn't open yet, and she had it all to herself as she wiped down tables and checked the bar stock.

THOMAS: Le Beau Series

The only problem was; it sometimes gave her too much time to think. Today was one of those times. She had her mother on her mind.

It wasn't that her mother didn't love her—she did. At least, she was pretty sure she did. But the woman had some pretty extreme ideas of late. She apparently believed shifters should only mate other born shifters, and humans were a scourge and diluted the bloodline.

In her disturbed mind, she believed if she dragged her daughters around to enough eligible shifter males, she could somehow force a pureblood mating.

Julia and Krystal were tired of being paraded before one shifter family after another. Tired of letting hundreds of males sniff them in the hopes of finding a mate. It was straight up embarrassing.

As much as she loved the bayou, she was seriously considering tagging along with Krystal to Lucas's ranch in Texas. She heaved a sigh and took a good, long look at the bar. All right, she would do it. If her mother tried to drag her out 'visiting' one more time, she'd pack up and head for Texas.

*****

It had been a busy shift at her bar The Backwater, and she was ready to relax in a bubble bath with a good romance novel.

Julia came through the front door of her home to a horrifying sight. Her beloved novels lay shredded and callously thrown in a pile. It must be her entire collection to create a mountain of pages and covers five feet high in her living room. Next to the carnage lay a note on a side table. The room smelled of anger, frustration, and her mother.

She was going to have to store her books in a safer place from now on. Huffing out an angry breath, she picked up the note.

You need to get your head out of the clouds and look for a mate. You won't find him in one of these human books. I've had it with your lack of interest in settling down. Pick out a mate, or I will pick one for you.

"Pick one for me? She has completely lost touch with reality."

Every shifter knew you couldn't just pick any old mate; you had to find the one who held the other half of your soul. It was time for a private talk with her father. He needed to know how crazy she was acting.

Sighing, at almost two hundred, she was well past the age by which she hoped to be mated. Every year her mother had marched available men into her quaint little house like she was presenting the latest fashions, or worse, dragged her to them. Not a single one had been her other half. How exactly was she to blame for that?

Then she read the last sentence of the note.

You will attend the dance at your Uncle Isaac's on Saturday. Perhaps this time you will find your mate.

Your Mother

She audibly groaned. She hated being sniffed by every single male who came within five feet of her. It made her feel dirty. The First thing she did after these setups was take a long, hot shower.

THOMAS: Le Beau Series

Julia thought back to the beginning of her 'shame', as her mother described it. She had gone to yet another event where she was set out like a prize to be won. When none of the men were a match, her parents informed her they were buying the Gator's Tooth Bar and Grill, and she would be the full-time bartender. Their hopes were she would stumble upon her mate amongst the patrons and visitors. The first thing Julia had done was rename the bar The Backwater to spite her mother.

Has it really been twenty years?

"Oh well, I have six days before Isaac's party; time enough to stock up on new books. And I'm not going to waste another second thinking about the party. Take that, Mother."

At least her uncle's party actually sounded fun. Her cousins would be there, and she could hang out with them while avoiding her mother.

The Day of the Gathering

Stretching, Julia considered what to do with her free day. The gathering didn't begin until seven that evening, and since everyone was invited, The Backwater was closed for the day.

Grabbing her robe, she slipped on her bunny slippers and made a beeline to the coffee maker. Goddess, she loved her new programmable machine. No more waiting for the coffee to brew for this girl.

Steaming cup in hand, she grabbed one of her new romance novels. A friend had recommended it, saying the storyline and names sounded like her cousin, Cade, and his mate, Anna. She'd never read V.A. Dold before, but she hoped it would be as good as her friend said it was.

Not two chapters into the book and the last person she wanted to see walked through her door. Her mother. Lucinda took one look at the book and turned an interesting color of purplish red.

"Do you always barge into a person's home without knocking?" Julia asked coolly.

"Where did you get that?"

"The coffee? From the pot in the kitchen."

"You know very well I'm not talking about the coffee."

"Well, if you're referring to my NEW book, touch it and die. And if you think I'm kidding, try it."

Lucinda was dumbstruck; Julia had never spoken to her like that before.

"Since I have a day of relaxation planned, why don't you tell me why you're here so I can get back to it?"

"I bought you a dress for the gathering. I was shopping for one for myself and saw this. It's your favorite color, and I'm sure it will be stunning on you." Lucinda held it out to Julia a little hesitantly.

Interesting. She'd never seen her mother unsure of herself.

I'm going to have to tell her off more often.

"I wasn't planning on wearing a dress, but I'll try it on later and see what I think of it."

"Wonderful. We'll pick you up at six thirty."

"No. You won't. I'm going by myself."

"But you have to ride with the family."

"Why?"

"Because that's the way you travel to these gatherings. You arrive as a family pack."

"Then I guess I'm starting a new tradition because I'm going by myself."

Lucinda narrowed her eyes. She was so mad, Julia checked to see if steam was rising out of her ears. "You wait until I tell your father."

"Go ahead. I'm still going by myself."

Lucinda growled, spun on her heel, and slammed the door on her way out.

"Well," Julia chuckled to herself, "that was pleasant."

Chapter 2

Thomas scowled at the crowd below. He had little patience for parties on his best day. And this wasn't even a good day.

The main yard was filling with family packs, as one after the other joined the celebration. Glancing to the right, he checked on the band doing a sound check. Near the rear of the designated party area, the caterer was busy filling the buffet table with every meat, salad, and dessert imaginable.

Scanning the milling crowd below, Thomas observed a woman moving through the throng of people. His position on the raised deck attached to the rear of his grandparent's house gave him the advantage of elevation. He scowled as his attention kept returning to her. Sure, she was pretty, and curvy, and sexy as hell, but he had a job to do. Besides, he avoided getting involved with women. Hookups – yes. Serious interest – no. Still, he felt the woman's presence and found himself staring at her again.

THOMAS: Le Beau Series

The yard was filling with shifters and humans visiting as they stood or sat at the beautifully decorated tables covered in linen. Males and their mates, most of whom she knew, circulated with cocktails in hand. This gathering had all the earmarks of the event of the season.

The only way to avoid her mother was to locate her first, so she scanned the area. That's when her gaze zeroed in on him. Julia stared in disbelief; it was like he had stepped off the pages of the novel she was reading. Her heart pounded so loudly; undoubtedly, anyone standing within ten feet could hear it. Attempting to swallow was more than difficult with a throat as dry as the Arizona desert. Even her lips were dry, which was crazy since she wore lip gloss. How was that possible in the humidity of the bayou? No man had ever had this effect on her before.

Her smile widened as she realized who he was. Thomas, Anna's son, the one Stefan mentioned at The Backwater. He had said Thomas was in charge of security for the royal family. This man must be him.

Her mother caught sight of her watching someone intently. She turned to see who'd managed to catch her daughter's interest and scowled. "He's human and far below your station as a lady in the royal family. Stay away from him."

Julia stepped away from Lucinda, unwilling to respond, and at the same time afraid of what her mother might do. Moving through the crowd nonchalantly, she made her way toward the new chief of security. It would be not only embarrassing but downright disastrous if her mother got wind of how deeply her interest went.

V.A. Dold

As she drew closer, his lean, hard body became more than evident. Goddess bless heightened wolf sight. The crisply ironed dress shirt and pleated slacks didn't have a chance in hell of disguising his well-developed, tanned chest and narrow waist. Clenching her hands, she controlled the urge to sprint to him and rip his shirt open, dying to know if his abs were as amazing as his chest appeared to be.

Upon closer inspection, his skin wasn't overly suntanned like some young humans tended toward, but more of a lovely tawny gold. Julia licked her lower lip as she spied the light dusting of dark hair hiding under his shirt. Biting her lip, she clenched her hands even tighter. Stupid hands. Stupid, stupid, hands.

Glancing at the parked cars, Thomas watched as yet another family emerged from an SUV. Cade immediately greeted the alpha and welcomed them. No threat there. Stefan joined Cade as Sam, a longtime friend of the family and foreman on the construction site for both Thomas and John's homes, arrived. His brow furrowed. Odd, something felt off about Sam.

"I need an update from each of you."

One by one, the men checked in with an "all clear."

Thomas had personally organized the handpicked security squad, each member equipped with an earpiece for coordinating the safety of the royal family. Someone was engineering accidents, and this huge gathering, out in the open, was a logistical nightmare. First, Stefan's mate, El, had her truck tampered with, so it would break down and expose her to an attack. Then his personal house was sabotaged while being built. An entire brick wall was rigged to fall on any person who stood below it.

THOMAS: Le Beau Series

When it triggered, the impact of the cement blocks almost killed Stefan.

He tried to talk Isaac into canceling the gathering, or at the very least moving the location, but Isaac insisted it be here in their seat of power.

For about the millionth time, he rubbed his burning stomach; his grandfather was giving him a damn ulcer. Sighing, he resigned himself to do the best he could with the situation he was stuck with.

Privately, Thomas grinned to himself. Isaac didn't know it, but he brought in a few of Simon's military buddies with sniper training and had them laying low in strategic positions around the party. Until recently, Simon had been unaware a few of his fellow servicemen were also shifters. For Thomas that new information came in rather handy.

A chuckle rumbled in his chest when Isaac gave him a small salute. His grandfather appreciated his ability to size up anyone; human or supernatural, made no difference. Little got past him and his gift, which was exactly why he'd been chosen to lead the security team.

Thomas returned to watching the party. It was dangerous to expose the king and queen to a multitude of possible attackers, no matter the location. And with a known threat existing against the royal family, the danger multiplied exponentially. The last thing he needed was a distraction, especially a female distraction, regardless of how beautiful and interesting she was.

Thomas had a well–earned reputation for sensing a threat. Whenever someone with criminal intentions was within a two–block radius of him, a frisson of awareness would make the back of his neck tingle and itch. It made it extremely uncomfortable to live in a city of any size.

Even a nasty fight between spouses could set his gift off, but he was getting better at blocking the lower level threats. This useful but sometimes annoying gift was just one of many reasons why he had moved from Denver, Colorado to the bayou.

Thomas pulsed the crowd again. Over the years he had honed his gift or was it a curse, he wasn't sure which, into a precision tool. With a little concentration, he could pinpoint the location of a person emitting a threat with unbelievable accuracy.

Rubbing his palm along the back of his neck, he attempted to ease the itch. There was a low–level threat within the crowd, but with the constant flow of bodies, and the almost imperceptible vibration, he couldn't target the source. The distraction of the fascinating woman wasn't helping either.

When he had described his strange ability to his grandfather, Isaac suggested perhaps he was sending out the equivalent of sonar waves once he sensed the threat thus allowing him to pinpoint it. An interesting concept, and one he'd explore further. But right now, hundreds of possible assassins milled around the estate.

Out of frustration, he tested the crowd again to see if the cause of his unease would present itself.

His personal distraction instantly raised her head and locked eyes with him.

Huh. That's interesting.

No one else noticed the low pulse of energy he emitted, except her. He knew she felt it by her expression.

She held him spellbound with her gaze for a long minute. Startled, the breath rushed from his chest. She hadn't touched him, heck, she was a good fifty yards

THOMAS: Le Beau Series

away, for God's sake, but he felt her palm on his cheek. With his lungs now completely devoid of air and chest constricted, he struggled to get another breath, the lack of oxygen making him lightheaded. His knees wobbled, and his lungs burned, reminding him to breathe. Worse yet, all the blood had rushed from his brain to lower regions. That was not helping him remain standing, not in the least.

He didn't dare look away in case the sensation of her hand stopped. Or continued. He was uncertain which he wanted. This reaction was completely unexpected and absolutely against his character. With his heart racing, he remained frozen beneath her invisible touch. The Strange thing was, he had no idea what he was waiting for.

Thomas puzzled out the situation. She wasn't a threat, at least not to his family. The worst she could do would be to rat him out about his gift. He felt like she'd bewitched him. And honestly, it annoyed him that she intrigued his curiosity and piqued his interest. He had no desire to have any woman peaking anything. Frowning in thought, he'd never met anyone who could feel the pulse when he emitted it. But now was not the time to examine that odd, new development.

He watched the golden-haired beauty continue to wade through the crowd. Try as he might, he couldn't take his eyes from her. Swallowing hard, he was torn between wanting to drag her away from the crowd and running in the opposite direction. Absently he cupped his jaw. He still felt her touch there, branded to his skin, and he had no idea how she'd managed it.

Shaking his head to clear it, he got back to work. There was no room in his life for women. After watching his parents' relationship, he realized that was not for him. Ever.

Using signals he'd taught his security team, he put them on alert. A hidden threat was the most dangerous. He couldn't position his team to strike if he didn't have a target. They were blind, sitting ducks, forced to wait for the assassin to make his or her move. Massaging the nape of his neck, he was once again relieved he assigned Cade, Simon, Lucas, and Marcus to remain within a five–foot radius of Isaac and Emma at all times. Let an assassin try to get past that wall of men.

The woman seemed to be making systematic passes through the crowd greeting each person as she went. With every step, she moved closer to where he stood–and increased the tightness of his slacks. He thrust his hand through the thick, damp curls lying against the moist skin of his neck. What was it about this woman that was causing such a strong reaction? He met beautiful women all the time without this level of awareness and distraction.

After growing up with his abusive father, he had no interest in relationships. Sure, he needed to scratch the itch like any red-blooded American male, but never more than once with the same woman. Second dates led to expectations.

One look into that woman's dark, velvety brown eyes sent his pulse tripping. A man could get trapped in those eyes, like Alice down the rabbit hole, and never find his way out. With that thought, he wanted to run for cover.

As he was considering his escape route, his senses went on full alert. A small group of partiers had wandered where they didn't belong, behind the house.

THOMAS: Le Beau Series

Thomas sent two men to herd them back into the party perimeter. He needed everyone where he could see them at all times.

Relentlessly scanning the crowd, another tingle shot up his neck. Every nerve went on high alert. His frustration mounted–it was still too faint, yet he found himself more certain than ever that something was off, and there was a traitor lurking in the crowd right under their noses.

"Everyone on high alert," Thomas said into their earpieces. "A threat is moving in the crowd but I haven't pinpointed it yet."

The threat remained hidden, within the party, as the wait staff began to serve dinner. Perhaps with the people sitting stationary, he would be able to locate the person responsible for his discomfort.

According to the schedule, Isaac was due to give a speech from the deck. At least he had been able to convince his grandfather to wear a bulletproof vest.

"What's the situation?" Isaac asked as he joined Thomas to take the microphone.

"Someone has been moving through the crowd. I haven't located him yet."

"All right, watch my back and I will try to make this short."

Thomas stepped back as Isaac called for everyone's attention.

"Welcome to the first annual shifter gathering. The reason for this celebration is twofold. First, I am announcing I am formally retaking the throne."

The crowd rose to their feet in a thunderous standing ovation.

V.A. Dold

"Thank you," Isaac said, waited for his guests to be seated once again. "Secondly, the elders requested I reinstate the annual gathering. Many of you younger people won't remember the old days when this was a regular occurrence. Due to the recent events of my sons finding their mates among human friends and family of existing shifters, I modified the guest list. I included all siblings and appropriate friends of our shifter community in hopes some of you will meet your mate tonight."

Another cheer rang through the crowd.

"I'm very excited to announce two of our men have already met their other half tonight. Please stand with your newly-found mates so we can toast you."

The entire party raised their glasses to the lucky couples.

"I sincerely hope more of you will meet your mate before the night is over. Please, enjoy your meal and the dance to follow. And thank you again for coming."

Isaac winked at him and took his seat.

Thomas frowned. *What is Grandpa up to?*

Thomas's tension was running high. Dinner had been cleared several minutes ago, and still no incident.

As the band prepared to play, he saw El walk onto the stage and take the microphone from the lead singer.

Quickly he adjusted the security team to cover her exposed position. They were definitely having a talk about safety after this party.

"Stefan Le Beau."

The crowd went silent waiting to see what was about to happen.

"I will give myself body and soul to complete you as a man and his wolf. I will unite my life with yours, bond my future to yours, and merge my half of our soul with yours. I will complete the mating ritual with you."

Stefan rushed the stage and snatched El off, laughing like a teenager in love.

Thomas breathed a little easier; at least she was no longer an open target.

*****

While the crowd had their attention on Stefan, the attacker made his move. Stealthy as a cat, he wove through the crowd until he was a mere six feet from the king. The assassin's boss instructed him to make it very public. It didn't get more public than this.

He'd hidden a razor sharp stiletto up his sleeve, so the moment he was close enough, he could drop it into his palm.

Casually, he spoke to the next person, greeting each as he stepped closer and closer. There was only Simon between him and his target.

Isaac's voice came through Thomas's earpiece. "Thomas, I smell him. His blood thirst is swamping me. Do you have him? I don't want to tear another shifter to shreds my first day as king."

Alarms clamored in Thomas's head, and the hair on the back of his neck was standing on end. He sent a single pulse. Instantly, his gaze shot to the perpetrator. "I have him, Grandpa. Don't move. Target located. The Man in the blue shirt, standing directly behind Simon, facing the king. Sniper, do you have the shot?"

"I have the shot."

"Take it."

A single shot rang out. Thomas watched the guests scramble as some of the crowd screamed while others dove for cover. All of the brothers converged on their parents.

"What?" Sam yelled as he tried to stop the bleeding. "Can't fight your own battles, old man?"

"I could easily allow you to shift and humiliate you if you so desire," Isaac responded calmly.

"You're just afraid to fight me and lose in front of an audience."

Isaac glanced at the faces nearest him. Skepticism permeated their regard. He sighed. "Fine. If you insist on further public shame..." Seconds later Isaac's massive black wolf stood in his place.

A struggle raged beyond the wall of bodies Thomas pushed through. He needed to be able to see the king and queen if he was going to keep them safe, but the crowd was too thick. He heard two wolves snarling savagely but couldn't see the fight. Finally, he squeezed through a hole in the circle to see one wolf limping on three legs, dragging the fourth behind, stupidly still ready to battle to the death. The other simply waited.

The instant Sam made his move, Isaac bore down on him, attacking and counterattacking over and over.

For a moment, black and white blurred. Then one pain–filled yelp rose above the din and silence fell as Sam's white wolf submitted.

Cade took control of Sam's wolf, allowing Isaac to shift back and force Sam to do the same.

With a nod from Thomas, Simon knelt next to the traitor, zip ties in hand, Cade still gripping the scruff of his neck like a dog.

El's gasp had Thomas turning her direction. She glanced wide–eyed at Stefan, then at the man again.

Slowly she pointed at Sam. "It's Joe. It was Joe the entire time."

"His name is Sam. Is this the man who attacked you?"

"Yes, but he told me his name was Joe."

"His real name," Stefan said, lifting Sam enough to smash a fist into his face, "is Sam." Stefan snarled, drew back his fist and drilled Sam in the stomach before Cade and Lucas restrained him.

Thomas directed the men to take Sam into custody.

"Good thinking, ordering a debilitating shot versus a kill shot, Thomas," Simon said, and then he glared at Stefan. "You can't question a dead man."

"I didn't kill him. Yet, anyway." Stefan snarled.

"You think this is over?" Sam spat blood on Isaac's shoe as he scanned the crowd. "We've only just begun. I wouldn't get too comfortable on that throne."

Thomas scowled at his behavior. He acted like he was looking for someone in particular.

"Get that trash out of here before I finish the job and rip him to shreds," Isaac whispered to Cade.

Cade and Simon held Sam and looked to Thomas for direction.

"Take him to a holding cell."

With a single nod, the men hauled Sam away from the party. He would be turned over to the interrogators for questioning. Every geographic area of the world had hand– selected and trained interrogators. The last thing a shifter who had committed a serious crime wanted was to be turned over to them. Talking wasn't an option.

Emma hugged Thomas tightly. "Thank you, baby."

"You're welcome, Grandma. Just doing my job. Speaking of which, I need to get back in position."

"Before you go, I have someone I want you to meet."

Thomas heaved a sigh. What was she up to?

"Julia?" Emma called over his shoulder to someone behind him. "Come over here, cher. I want you to meet Thomas."

As he turned to politely greet Julia, he came face to face with the woman he had stared at in the crowd.

Ah, hell.

"Ma'am." Thomas nodded his greeting.

Julia...what, a beautiful name, and it fit her perfectly. He had an insane desire to whisper it over and over as he licked and nibbled her neck.

What the hell! Where are these crazy urges coming from?

She offered him a small, shy smile, her gaze flicking to his nervously. The moment their eyes met, he felt the impact like a punch to his stomach. When her hand accidentally brushed his, he stopped breathing altogether.

"It's nice to meet you, Thomas."

Her voice sang like an electric current through his veins. No one had ever had this effect on him before.

What's wrong with me?

Normally he was the poster boy for common sense. But he swore as he stood staring at the most beautiful woman he'd ever met, common sense waved bye–bye wearing a shit–eating grin.

*****

There was something magnetic about him, drawing her in. A cloud of toe-curling dark spices swamped her senses as her feet propelled her closer of their own accord. The intense effect of his scent rocked her sharply. Startled, she had to grab his arm to keep from falling. She watched as concern filled his gaze while he steadied her against his chest. With wide eyes, she stopped. Suspended in time. Staring in shock.

MATE!

Her wolf howled over and over, as it recognized its other half. Tail wagging and body quivering in anticipation of meeting Thomas's wolf.

*****

The closer she came, the more panicked he became. And that rather pissed him off. Nervously, he glanced at his grandmother, and then about, to make sure no one was a witness to this fiasco.

His eyes narrowed as she swayed into him. Just as he was on the verge of excusing himself; the dang woman up and tripped or something. Instead of creating a distance between them, he found himself pulling her against his chest to steady her. Air rushed into his body and took in a scent that had no business in the bayou.

What was happening to him? He didn't know. He wasn't sure he wanted to know, but he wanted it to stop. Thomas didn't trust relationships, and this held all the earmarks of that possibility.

Each time her eyes met his, a peculiar twinge fluttered in the pit of his stomach, very slight, but the sensation was uncomfortable and made it difficult to think. It didn't help when her dark eyes drifted over his body like a tangible touch. Worse, she took the very air from his lungs. Damn, he was actually getting lightheaded.

V.A. Dold

Julia stood frozen in place by Thomas's intense gaze and the fact she just heard him say "Ah, hell" in her mind. The moment his incredible blue gaze caught hers, her pulse leapt. There was enough heat in his stare to ignite a forest fire. Neither she nor Thomas moved or spoke for what felt like minutes. As he devoured her with his eyes, a shiver shook her body. The intense energy flowing between them seared her to the core.

Carefully, Julia slipped out of his embrace, and moved around a nearby table to put the solid piece of furniture between them, and hopefully conceal the unnatural awareness growing with every passing second. Her heart thundered a hard, erratic rhythm that assured her she was in deep doo–doo. By mating a human, she was breaking all her mother's rules.

Standing as tall as possible, she tried to mask her reaction, but she was sure she failed epically. God forbid her mother see the effect he had on her. Navigating these waters would require covertness. But dang, defying her mother, actually excited her. Her sister, Krystal, was going to have a good laugh over this, and she'd be all over helping her see Thomas behind their mother's back.

Mother is going to have a coronary when she finds out my mate is human.

Chapter 3

From his vantage point, Thomas watched as Cade and Simon returned. Sam was on ice, but for some reason there was still an undercurrent of malice.

Great.

In his mind, two things were possible. Either someone was angry about Sam's arrest or there might be another attack before the night was over. As Thomas considered this, he pulsed the party, but, like before, he was unable to locate the source.

"Grandpa, there's still someone within the crowd, but I think you're safe to get the festivities going again. But, please, stay very aware of anyone near you while I stay on top of the situation, and if you could manage it, stop the improv. I can't protect you if I have no idea what you will do next."

"Copy that," Isaac responded, then he grabbed a microphone on stage. "Please excuse the interruption. The situation has been handled. Let the dancing begin! Hit it, boys."

V.A. Dold

The drummer hammered out a wild riff as the lead singer took the microphone and the band members grabbed their instruments.

Isaac got the party going again, and Cade, Simon, and Stefan were on the dance floor.

Thomas watched as Stefan pulled El in for a kiss and instantly searched for Julia in the crowd.

Shit, I'm so screwed.

*****

About twenty minutes later, Isaac took the stage and waited for the crowd to quiet before he spoke.

Thomas grumbled into the earpiece. "Everyone stay on your toes, there is still a threat and Isaac is in the open."

Isaac glanced at Thomas and chuckled, then continued to address the party. "I and my mated sons have a special song for our beloved mates. Cade, Simon, and Stefan, come on up."

Each of the mated Le Beau men positioned their women in the front row and hopped on stage.

Thomas about had a heart attack. "Dang it, Grandpa." This was turning into a nightmare.

Once the men were lined up on stage, each with a cordless microphone, the band began the lead in chords of *I Cross My Heart* by George Strait.

"Our love is unconditional, we knew it from the start." All four men had perfect pitch and harmonized flawlessly.

Thomas vaguely wondered if a good singing voice was part and parcel of being a shifter, like being attractive seemed to be. One thing he didn't have was a good singing voice.

THOMAS: Le Beau Series

As they sang the second line, they filed down the stage stairs to stand before each of their mates. As the men reached the first chorus, "I cross my heart and promise to give all I've got to give to make all your dreams come true," each dropped to one knee.

Gasps were heard throughout the audience as every mated male in the crowd got down on one knee before his mate and joined in the song.

As they sang, Thomas located Julia sitting off to the side of the party. Like before, they locked eyes and were unable to look away. He was mesmerized. It was like having tunnel vision, and the only thing he saw was her.

As much as he wanted to stare at her until the end of time, his family was in danger. Tearing his gaze away, he returned to check the guests for threats.

With the last note fading into silence, the men stood and gathered their mates into their arms. Happy tears and sniffles were heard throughout the crowd. The unmated males watched with happiness and yearning etched on their faces. Like them, he wanted a mate, too.

Where the heck did that come from?

As he watched from above, Thomas saw El kiss Stefan and head toward their house by herself.

"John, you have El until she returns."

"Copy that."

Stefan paced like a caged animal. It looked like he was waiting for her to return. Then suddenly, Stefan took off for home.

"John, you see Stefan?"

"On it." John climbed down from his location in a nearby tree and repositioned outside Stefan's house.

After quite a while, El came out the front door with a rumpled and unhappy Stefan in tow. He grumbled something unintelligible as he poofed on clothing on the front lawn.

Once they had cleared the tree line and entered the well–lit party, John returned to his original position.

Grandma Emma was clapping excitedly as Grandpa Isaac bounded onto the stage. Now, what were they up to! He really needed to have a conversation with these people about preparation. How was he supposed to keep them safe if they kept veering off the planned course?

"Everyone, please take a seat. We have a wedding to witness."

Thomas frowned in confusion as he watched Stefan stare at his father, and then look at El, who was grinning back at him.

She pulled what looked like a ring from her pocket and took his hands.

"Stefan Le Beau, will you marry me? Right here? Right now?"

"Hell, yes!"

The crowd erupted in cheers while Thomas buried his face in his hands and groaned.

A minister joined the happy couple on stage, and from the back of the crowd, Cade led El's grandmother Marie to join her as maid of honor.

The gathering quickly transformed into a wedding reception, which, of course, Thomas had known nothing about. A cake appeared on the buffet table, and waiters offered champagne glasses to the guests.

"Are you people trying to kill me?" Thomas snarled into the earpieces.

"Oh, stop fussing and come get a piece of cake," Emma laughed.

THOMAS: Le Beau Series

"Grandma, you realize we are going to have a serious chat, right?"

"Whatever you say, cher."

Thomas threw his hands in the air in frustration. He might as well give up now. Before he joined the party to congratulate Stefan and El, he pulsed the crowd again. Not a single thread of anger or malice returned. Whoever had been a threat must have left. Good, now he could breathe easier.

The moment Stefan and El headed home again, the band took the stage for a few songs to celebrate the nuptials before the formal toast. Lucas yelled, "Devil Went Down to Georgia," and about thirty people lined up for the line dance.

"Do we need to stay on guard, boss?" John asked.

"Come on in, men, and enjoy the reception, the threat is gone."

As the security contingent filled their plates with food, Lucas leapt on stage, raised his hands, and waited for the crowd to quiet down.

"Stefan has been blessed by our Goddess with an incredible woman. She's tough as nails and solid as a rock. My brother is a damn lucky man to have her as his mate." Lucas raised his glass. "Let us raise our glasses in a toast to Stefan and El."

The band raised their glasses along with the crowd. Then everyone shouted, "To Lord Stefan and Lady El. May they live a long and happy life together."

Every empty glass was then banged on the tabletops three times.

Once the crowd quieted again, Lucas replaced the microphone in its stand and held up his right arm. The instant he dropped it to his side, every shifter in the place changed to their wolf form. Wolves of every color and size stood where the party guests had been. Humans remained scattered amongst the pack of black, brown, white, gray, and every shade in between.

Where Lucas had been, a gray and white wolf peppered with black now stood. With a yip, Lucas leapt from the stage and raced around the bandstand toward the woods. Every wolf raced after him. An eerie chorus was heard from the pack as it faded into the forest and disappeared from sight.

Thomas slowly surveyed the remaining humans. He still didn't sense a threat, and as the band began to play, many enjoyed the dance floor.

Turning to retake his post on the deck, he found a fairly large, cream–colored wolf gazing at him with its head cocked.

"Shouldn't you be with the pack?"

Julia shivered, his voice was deep and rich. So mesmerizing, it sent an electrified zing up her spine.

Thomas swallowed hard as Julia's wolf moved into an area aglow with the full moon. The radiance made her fur shimmer. She was just as beautiful in this form as she was human. Her coat looked so silky smooth; he had to stop his hands from reaching for her. The need to touch her was making his palms itch. It baffled him that he knew it was her, how could he have possibly known that?

He rubbed his hands through his thick dark hair to occupy them before he truly embarrassed himself. When the wolf became Julia, the sudden change made him instinctively take a step back. Dang it, he'd get used to their shifting one of these days.

"No, I changed my mind and decided to stay here." She tentatively held her hand out. "Would you dance with me, Thomas?"

He was about to say no, he was busy and didn't have time to waste dancing when his damn hand accepted hers.

What am I doing?

Her skin was softer than anything he'd ever felt. With a bit of effort, he managed to pause his hand before he cupped her cheek. For some crazy reason, he wanted to run his fingers across that cheek. Repeatedly, and explore every part of her luscious body.

And her perfume...it was freshly fallen snow! She smelled fresh, crisp, and clean; like a winter morning in Denver. It was all he could do not to bury his nose in her hair and bask in it. A scowl creased his brow as her heat, and the scent surrounded him.

They make the weirdest perfumes these days.

It was like World War Three inside his heart and mind as he fought an inner battle with himself. Thomas wanted to kiss her so badly he could taste it. He decided right then; this woman was an absolute menace and must be avoided. But he knew that wasn't going to happen.

Squaring his shoulders, he led her to the dance floor, praying he wouldn't trip or step on her toes. *Note to self; thank Mom for making me take a few dance lessons.* Never in his life had he ever expected to thank her for that.

Julia's folly became all too clear the moment he gripped her hip as they joined the waltzing couples.

He's going to feel how chubby I am!

The dress her mother insisted she wear, left nothing to the imagination. Why couldn't designers make flattering clothes for plus-sized women? It was bad enough everyone could see her less than ideal size sixteen figure. She cringed when his palm slipped higher to her waist, knowing his hand was on her squishy, marshmallow waistline, feeling how thick and flabby it was.

Thomas wanted to run his hands all over her body and relish her curves. She was absolute perfection. How had he managed to end up on the dance floor holding this beautiful woman? She was everything he had ever wanted. Her beauty mesmerized him, and her sweet, shy smile tugged at his heart. She drew him in and terrified him at the same time.

"Are you enjoying the gathering?"

"Yes." Julia chuckled. "It's been rather interesting."

"Do you mean the issue with Sam?"

"No." She shook her head and laughed. "Way more interesting than that."

"What do you mean?"

"Well, remember the king saying he hoped others would find their mate tonight?"

He hesitated and drew back. "Yeah..."

"I found mine."

"Oh, shit." Thomas stepped away from her. "I'm sorry, I shouldn't be dancing with you then."

Julia frowned with her hands on her hips. "Why not?"

"A man doesn't go around dancing with another man's mate."

Her hand flew to her mouth, as her eyes grew large. Then she whispered. "You don't realize, do you?"

Thomas frowned. "Realize what?"

"Maybe we should talk somewhere private."

THOMAS: Le Beau Series

"No. It's never a good idea to get cozy with the mate of a shifter male." He stepped even further away. "And all males are crazy until the ritual is completed. Heck, even after the ritual they're off their rockers where their mates are concerned."

She covered her mouth and giggled, and there was a mischievous twinkle in her eyes that he didn't understand at all.

"Are you saying you feel a bit crazy?"

Now he was really confused. "Not in the least. Why?"

"Because it's you."

"It's me…what?"

"Oh, good Goddess." She sighed. "I'll say this really slow for you. You. Are. My. Mate."

Thomas literally gaped at her. Mouth hanging open. Huge eyes. Drool down the chin. Gaped.

Julia was beginning to worry. "Are you okay?"

"I…I don't think I heard you right. Did you just say I'm your mate?"

"Yes." She laughed. "Yes, I did."

"How is that possible? I thought that only worked for human women and shifter males."

"It goes the other way as well. It's just a lot more rare."

"When's the last time this" – he waved between them – "happened?"

"Actually." Julia looked away sheepishly. "I haven't heard of it happening in my lifetime."

"So… how do you know we are mates? How can you be so sure?"

Julia blushed a bright red. "I think I would know my mate and the signs."

"Oh." Thomas ducked his head.

"Maybe we should just finish our dance for now?"

Thomas's expression turned to one of relief. "Good idea."

With each sway of her hips, he fell a little further under her spell. Swamped by stronger feelings than he ever expected to feel for any woman. But then, he'd never had a mate before.

He wasn't sure he was at all comfortable with the whole situation.

When the song ended, he stepped away, intending on returning to his post as quickly as possible.

Julia had other ideas. Faster than he could react, she wrapped her arms around his neck and planted a kiss on his lips. The shock of it had him staggering back and confused beyond words.

Chapter 4

"Hey Junior," Marcus grinned as he turned to glance at Thomas, mischief twinkling in his eyes. "I know a gal I wanted to set you up with."

"What?" Thomas gave Marcus an annoyed look. "I had a long night and it's too early in the morning for your shit."

"Not shit, a girl, you moron. I have one for you to take out on a date."

"Not interested, buddy."

"And why is that? You have someone else occupying your time?"

"Spit it out, Marcus," Thomas growled. "What are you getting at?"

Marcus forced his expression to remain uninterested. "Nothing, I thought you might like to meet this awesome gal I met the other night and take her on a date."

"I don't need you or anyone else setting me up. I have someone."

"Really? Since when?"

V.A. Dold

Thomas scowled at Marcus. "Stop playin' me, dude. I know you, and everyone else saw me."

Marcus barked out a belly laugh, which startled everyone within hearing distance. He wasn't known for laughing or joking around.

"Oh, shut up," Thomas snarled.

He'd managed to concentrate on reviewing the night's events and security issues that needed addressing without thoughts of Julia intruding. At least for the last thirty minutes. Thanks to Marcus his concentration just waved good–bye again, laughing hysterically as it went.

"So. Since you have a gal hid away somewhere, you won't mind if I set my cousin up with a friend of mine?" He just had to keep poking the sleep deprived, surly man. It was too fun to let pass by.

Bad idea.

Very bad idea.

Thomas's expression went dark, dangerous, right before he launched himself onto Marcus's back and started pummeling the ignorant idiot.

"Hey! What's your problem, man?"

"Keep. Your. Horny. Buddies. Away. From. My. Mate!" Thomas emphasized each word with a punishing blow.

Marcus managed to loosen Thomas's grip enough to throw him off. "Krystal is your mate?"

Thomas looked like a Mac truck had blindsided him. "Krystal?"

"Well, yeah. Who did you think I was talking about?"

"Are you telling me you honestly didn't see me last night?" Thomas panted.

"No, I saw you with Julia." Marcus clarified,

rubbing his jaw as a big grin spread across his face "But I was talking about Krystal."

When Thomas remained silent, Marcus took a good look at his nephew and found a glaze-eyed smitten fool.

"Oh, son. You should see your expression," Marcus snickered, hand cupping Thomas's shoulder. "You, my friend, are irreversibly whipped."

*****

Eight a.m. and Julia was back at the Royal Plantation. Heat warmed her face along with all her intimate parts further south, the ones she'd already decided to ignore. What was the point, until Tommy accepted they were mates, her libido was on lock down.

Dang it! I need to think of something other than...him. Stupid horny body!

Granted, she'd only had a small sample of what being with him would be like when he danced with her at the gathering. And then there was the kiss – she'd wanted so much more than one dance and an unexpected kiss, but she would take what she could get for now.

Hopefully, it had been enough to get his attention. If that small sample of their explosive passion did its job, he would be courting her in no time. At least that's how it happened in her books.

Please, let it be like my books, she thought as she began to daydream about him, for oh, the thousandth time.

He'd looked exactly the way she imagined the heroes in her stories. Wide, strong shoulders, muscled arms and legs. Solid, but not overly muscled to the point of looking creepy, like some guys on steroids and a billion hours in the gym. A trim waist with what she

V.A. Dold

imagined was a delicious, defined abdomen and chest.

Enough swooning over the man, she was here to see Aunt Emma. Somehow she had left her Michael Kors® clutch behind last night. It couldn't have had anything to do with the way Tommy scrambled her brain. No, not at all.

Why did her brain take an exotic vacation every time she thought about the sheriff? She figured since he was in charge of security for her uncle, the shifter King, Sheriff, was a fitting title, so that was what she called him.

Maybe it was his incredible, shy smile? Or it could be his heart melting sky blue eyes? But there was his smoking hot body too. It could be that. No. No, it was most certainly his sexy, 'in charge' energy, and completely confident personality.

Oh, what the heck. It's the whole dang package.

Her complete lack of concentration or control of her wayward daydreaming wasn't just because of his looks. If it were, she would be a blubbering idiot every night at The Backwater. There was nothing but wall–to–wall hotness everywhere she looked. Total gorgeousness, with a capital G. But she had no trouble functioning around that crowd of panty incinerating men, heck she bossed them around on a nightly basis without batting an eyelash.

It had to be the mating attraction blasting her with all its might. The Goddess must really want to get them together in a hurry.

As much as she enjoyed her little erotic dreams of Tommy, she really needed her brain firing on all cylinders. She couldn't function when it took a hike into the land of naked Tommy bliss. It's a wonder she didn't walk into oncoming traffic and get hit by a bus. Until she convinced him to complete the ritual, she was a hazard to herself and anyone who came within a hundred feet of her.

A Movement to her left caught her eye as she stepped from her car. It looked like her cousins were taking a coffee break on Simon's patio. From what she could see, all of them were there. She swore someone else sat with them, and her heart skipped a beat. Was that Tommy? But the angle was wrong so that she couldn't be sure. She waved back at her beloved trouble making cousins as she reached the front steps.

Aunt Emma pulled the door open before she could knock. "Julia! Good morning, cher. I'm so glad you could come over so quickly. I bet a certain security guard is happy to see you, too."

"Thomas?" she frowned and then narrowed her gaze on her aunt. "I wouldn't know. I haven't spoken to him. The question is, what do you know about it Aunt Emma?"

"Oh, nothing. It's just the way he looked at you last night," she hedged, a knowing smile curving her lips as her eyes twinkled.

"Right..." Julia drew out the word sarcastically. "You haven't been matchmaking have you?"

"Me?" Emma clutched her chest dramatically and gasped for good measure. "I would never. But mark my words; he's interested in you. I've never seen him so taken by a woman."

Julia crossed her arms. "Somehow, I don't believe you. Regardless, I'm here to get my purse, not flirt with Thomas."

"Of course, you are," Emma said patting Julia's

arm. "I was just making tea. Would you like to have a cup with me before you go?"

"Yes, please. I'd love a cup."

*****

Thomas sipped his coffee, relieved to have a busy schedule today. Between his duties to the king as head of security and Jack and Michael returning after their conversion to vampire, he'd hardly spared a thought for Julia.

Just the thought of his long time friends, Jack, and Michael took him back to that fated day in the bayou. Rose had been abducted, and they were taking her back.

Sadly, during the battle with the shifters who snatched Rose, Jack and Michael had been mortally wounded.

Thomas remembered that day as clearly as if it were yesterday.

I had watched as Simon hissed into Travis's ear, demanding to know where Rose was. The menace in Simon's growl spoke of the long, painful death he had planned for this idiot.

Travis told my uncle Simon to go to hell, blood pouring down his face and soaking his torn shirt. He had even spat teeth before he threw back his head and laughed like a crazy man. But when Travis had claimed, "She's long gone, and you're never gonna find her." I couldn't breathe.

Uncle Simon's attack on Travis, his overwrought roar, and wild slashing shocked me back to reality.

Travis tried to shift but couldn't. That's when Grandpa really floored me. He can stop a shifter from changing!

THOMAS: Le Beau Series

Grandpa Isaac calmly stood before that maniac and said, "You can't shift unless I will it." Dang, Grandpa, is badass.

That was when it got really bad. Travis broke free and lunged at Michael and Jack with a knife. Michael blocked the initial attack, taking a gash to his arm. That was when Jack put Travis in a chokehold. I had never seen anyone escape one of Jack's holds before, but Travis was slick with blood and Jack's grip slipped.

Before Stefan could get ahold of Travis, he managed to slash Michael across his belly, and Jack across the throat.

Thomas shivered as he remembered the agonized scream that had torn from Michael's throat. His guts actually spilled into his hands. It was no wonder he went into shock.

Then that bastard turned on me. Wrong move asshole. I was more than ready for him. I blew his chest open with a slug from my shotgun. When he kept coming, I flipped him to the ground.

The idiot was too stupid to stay down. He tried to get to his knees, and Rose came out of nowhere and took that idiot out with a rock! It was awesome!

Rose couldn't handle losing her brothers and begged Etienne to save them.

Even though, Michael was white as a sheet and scarcely breathing. Rose managed to get both of them to agree to be turned into vampires.

Who knew Rose could be so demanding? Suddenly she was shouting commands and directions. She even started yelling commands at Etienne.

A bulldozer couldn't have moved that determined woman. She stood there and watched the entire process while Etienne fed both Jack and Michael his blood, careful not to give them too much.

Etienne let us know it would take time for the men to recover and be ready to be around humans. At the time, none of us really knew what he meant by that.

The time to learn to be a vampire in modern day society that Etienne had spoken of, took months. But they were finally ready to join the security team for the king.

Shaking off the memories of that terrible day, Thomas tried to think of something more pleasant. He told himself he wasn't imagining Julia's soft curves, or hot sweet mouth, and certainly not her incredible scent…

Shit. Who was he kidding? He hadn't stopped thinking about her. Hell, he hadn't slept a wink fantasizing about her in his bed.

Out of habit, his gaze roved continuously, taking in his surroundings, his vigilance was why he saw her car pull up to the main house. Luckily, she hadn't seen him. His heart seized before it nearly pounded its way clean through his chest. Damn, his ribs actually hurt, from the beating they'd just received.

Was she going to cause this reaction every time he saw her? He sure hoped not.

Thomas tried to force himself not to stare. That was a losing battle; he couldn't tear his gaze away.

Licking his lips, he focused on her bare neck. He loved the way she wore her long hair swept up in a messy bun thingy. His fingers itched to twirl the dangling tendrils around them.

Thomas's heart slammed hard in his chest once again trying to batter his ribs to dust. With five of the brothers sitting at the table with him, he couldn't afford to let them catch him ogling their cousin. Carefully, he kept his face expressionless, utilizing his years of practice around his psychotic father. As children, if he or John showed any emotion, their father immediately preyed on them. If they were happy, he would make them miserable. If they were sad, he would rub salt in the wound. The man was straight up evil. And when it came to Julia, he'd never been so attracted or aware of anyone in his life, and his emotions were all over the board.

"Hey, Thomas, look," Lucas said as he elbowed him. "There's your girly friend."

The pain–in–his–ass waved at his cousin, but it must be his lucky day because she didn't notice.

"Since when are you dating Julia?" Stefan asked, feigning ignorance as he joined Lucas waving and laughing like a hyena.

The ruckus the guys were causing caught her attention. She smiled and waved back. When she acted like she hadn't seen him, he breathed a sigh of relief. That was a bullet dodged. He wondered if his grandparents would notice a couple of their son's missing. Glaring at Lucas and Stefan, he decided it might be worth the risk.

"Congratulations, you lucky dog. I have to tell you; there are going to be a lot of heartbroken shifters at The Backwater when word gets around about you two." As Cade spoke, Thomas's expression and behavior finally registered. Something was off. "I thought she was your mate?"

Who has the hot's for my woman?

Where the hell did that thought come from?

He opened his mouth to ask who he needed to beat the crap out of, but then noticed Cade scowling at him. Had he asked him something?

"What's that?"

"I asked you if Julia was your mate."

"Yeah, well...Maybe. But I don't do relationships so let's drop the subject."

Simon walked out of the kitchen with a fresh pot of coffee and a bottle of brandy. Grinning, he poured an even mix into Thomas's cup. "You look like you could use a little encouragement."

Marcus snorted, but wisely kept his mouth shut. Smart man.

Lucas smirked. "Sure you do. You're just in denial. But that's okay. Simon had the same delusions when he met his mate, Rose. Look at him now. Your stupidity will pass soon enough."

Simon smacked Lucas on the back of the head as Stefan rubbed his hands together like an excited little boy. "Well, since you're not interested, I'll let all the guys know she's still available. Some of my friends wanted an introduction."

Thomas stood so fast his chair toppled to the floor. "Back off, asshole."

Both Lucas and Stefan barked out laughs as Cade held Thomas back from killing his dimwit brothers.

"Knock it off, you idiots, or I'll let him have a go at you."

The guys attempted to maintain straight faces but it only resulted in more laughter.

"That's enough, both of you. Go and make yourselves useful cleaning up the party."

"I thought the party supplier was doing that," Stefan whined.

"They were. But now, you're doing it."

Pouting like spoiled children, Stefan and Lucas left the meeting. When it came to a challenge, no one was stupid enough to push Cade.

"Take your seat, Thomas." Cade gave him the do what I tell you or else, stare. "We need to review what worked and what didn't last night for security. That should take your mind off things...but we're going to have a chat about your mate afterward."

Thomas didn't say it out loud, but he had no plans of discussing Julia with Cade or anyone else for that matter.

He didn't need nor want his advice. He was fine just the way he was. Single, unattached, and unmated.

Cade narrowed his piercing gaze on Thomas. "Whatever bright idea you just had...you're wrong. If you think you don't need your mate, you're doubly wrong. And take it from Simon and me, if you think you can control this situation...you might as well give up right now because you are completely and utterly helpless to prevent your relationship with Julia."

Thomas shook his head. "This isn't the same thing as your situations."

Marcus, who had sat silently during the exchange, threw his head back and laughed. "Oh, man. This is going to be a good show."

Simon ignored Marcus and leaned toward Thomas. "You have a lot to learn about mates, and believe me, you're going to learn the hard way if you maintain that attitude."

V.A. Dold

How the hell had he ended up the topic of conversation? Thomas slammed his empty coffee mug down and glared at the three do–gooders staring at him.

Shaking with frustration, he took a deep breath and a moment to calm himself. "Look, I'm sure you mean well, but drop it." Then he turned to Cade. "You know my history with my father. I don't do relationships. Don't get me wrong, I'm happy for you and Mom but settling down, and a family isn't in the cards for me. I don't want a wife or a mate. That's just the way it is."

Marcus suddenly leaned back in his chair; the creaking drew Thomas's attention. Marcus was looking at something over his shoulder with a sad expression on his face. Slowly he turned, and son–of–a–bitch, Julia stood not two feet away, white as a sheet.

Ah hell.

"Excuse me, I didn't mean to interrupt. You all have a good day."

Julia turned on her heel so fast she almost lost her balance. The tears filling her eyes didn't help either.

"Julia?" He didn't know what to say or how to apologize.

She snapped back around to face him. Fists clenched and heaven help him, righteous indignation flared in her usually soft brandy colored eyes.

The woman was scary when she was mad. Breathtaking, but damn, she scared the crap out of him with that angry expression aimed his way.

He'd heard many times that one mate could feel the others emotions and even see images sent to them through the telepathic bond, but it was freaking creepy to actually experience it the first time.

THOMAS: Le Beau Series

He knew the emotions he felt crushing his chest were hers.

Unconsciously, he rubbed the heel of his hand over the ache and tried to form words. He'd hurt her badly and for some reason his heart broke as well. Dang it, he couldn't think clearly when it came to her, much less, form a complete sentence.

"Please, let me apologize..."

"Why, Tommy? Do you suddenly feel differently?"

Her voice, though only a whisper, was filled with emotion, and it sent a frisson of desire through his entire body. Longing replaced the ache in his chest and swirled in his belly. He felt her whisper all the way to his toes. No one had ever dared call him Tommy before, but when she did, he kind of liked it.

Awareness hit him like a freight train. When had she crept into his heart so deeply he knew there was no chance of his walking away?

Stepping to her, he ran his hands through his hair, the confusion evident in his eyes. "Yeah, I guess I do feel differently."

Her lashes fluttered like she was trying to prevent tears from falling, and he found himself gazing into two deep pools of rich brandy. The jolt almost knocked him on his ass. The woman was downright dangerous; she didn't even need to touch him to bring him to his knees.

Like steel to a magnet, she drew him in. He couldn't stop himself from pulling her close and brushing her lips gently with his own. His body immediately went on alert, his erection was instantaneous and urgent.

A shy smile slowly curved her lips. Evidently she felt his condition against her belly as well.

To hell with the audience they had, he needed more than one small kiss. Wrapping his hand around the nape of her neck, he growled into her ear, "I need you to kiss me right now, Julia."

The demand was guttural with need. He'd never been so turned on in his life. He hadn't believed it was possible for him to feel this strongly for a woman.

Without a word, she raised her face to his.

His kiss was fierce and a claiming in and of itself. He wanted to kiss her forever. But that wasn't logical, eventually they had to come up for air.

With one last, soft kiss, he lifted his head.

Julia smiled at him, a gentle, sweet smile. Holy hell, just her smile had his body hard enough to pound nails.

Comprehension dawned, and silently he admitted to himself, one lifetime, even a shifter's long life of fourteen hundred years, wasn't long enough to spend with her.

Whoa. What the hell am I thinking? Dating, yes. Mating the woman, that's a wait and see, kind of thing.

He looked off into the distance as if he were considering something, and then nodded almost imperceptibly, as if agreeing with himself.

Julia's pulse skipped as she watched a slow grin tug at Tommy's kissable lips. And here she thought he was handsome when he was grouchy. This man with his sexy smile was utterly gorgeous. The transformation was nothing short of shocking, in a very arousing way.

Thomas felt nervous and awkward as he considered dating Julia, heck, dating any woman, but ten times less sure of himself with her. Relationships were so foreign to him, he was used to being in charge, calling the shots, and with this situation he was a fish out of water. If she needed him to arrest someone, no problem, but dating, and, God forbid, romance? That was something altogether different.

Julia kept her face averted as she tried not to giggle at his thoughts and anguish. His reaction was hilarious, but there was no way she was going to react. His feelings of inadequacy were endearing and downright sweet.

It was obvious he didn't realize she just heard his thoughts. It was amusing that he thought he could actually fight or control the mating bond. But, for now, she would let him believe he had some control over the situation.

His piercing blue gaze returned to her. Once again, Julia felt the impact all the way to her toes. Intense. Powerful. Captivating.

She waited for him to speak, his gaze searching her eyes and moving over her face. Uncertainty darkened his eyes as he eased his hold and cleared his throat.

"Would you mind if John and I came to The Backwater tonight?" Quickly he added, "To review your security procedures, of course."

"I would love to have you guys come out." *Check security, my butt.*

He cleared his throat again. "Good. Then I'll see you tonight."

He reached for her hand, sliding his fingers over hers, in a casual caress. Her gaze locked with his, and she knew there must be a million questions dancing in her eyes. His gaze never left hers as he brought her palm to his chest. The gesture made her heart rejoice in a thunderous pounding ovation. It may take a little time, but he was coming around.

She could feel his passionate need to protect her. Defending the people he loved was so deeply ingrained in his nature. She wondered if he realized that about himself.

"Would you like to join us for a cup of coffee?"

"I would love to."

Julia preceded him to the patio table where her cousins still sat. Amazingly they had managed to keep their normal snarky comments to themselves during her and Tommy's exchange. She shot a quick glance at Tommy as she took her seat. She couldn't help herself, her eyes were just naturally drawn to him.

Thomas's heart skipped a beat when he caught her looking his way.

She could knock the thoughts right out of his head when she looked at him like that. Having studied her at the gathering and again this morning, he had the feeling Julia was a woman who could handle herself. He couldn't put his finger on why he felt that way, but he did. Regardless, it didn't stop him from needing to protect her. From life? From the guys at the bar? He had no idea what he was protecting her from, he just had this bone-deep need to make sure she was safe.

He flung his arm casually around the back of her chair as Simon poured her a cup of coffee.

"Good morning, cher," Cade said grinning at her and then Thomas.

Chapter 5

She was enjoying the coffee and company, but Julia had a full day and she really needed to get going.

She finished her last sip and set her cup on the table. "Thank you for the coffee, Simon. And I'll see you and John tonight," she said to Thomas.

Thomas rose with her as she stood to go.

"I'll walk you to your car."

The stroll across the yard was a quiet one. Neither spoke. She hoped this awkward phase would pass quickly.

Julia exhaled a nervous breath. "I'd really like to get to know you better, Tommy."

"I would like to get to know you, too." Thomas grinned broadly. "Can I take you out tonight?" He asked, completely forgetting the ruse of checking her security.

"I need to open the bar but I'll be off by eight or so. Will that work?"

"Works for me. Is it okay if I come to The Backwater and hang out until you're ready to leave?"

Julia smiled brightly. "I'd like that."

V.A. Dold

Thomas held the car door for her. Once she was belted in, he leaned forward and captured her lips. He hadn't meant to give her more than a gentle good–bye kiss. Needless to say, it didn't go as planned. Ten minutes later he was finally waving good–bye as she pulled away.

Shaking her head, Julia attempted to rid her brain of the mind numbing fog Thomas caused every time he kissed her. Focusing her eyes on the road and gathering her scattered wits, she managed to make the turn to her private dock on her first try. It could be a real hassle to maintain a dock space on the mainland and live in the swamp, but she loved it.

*****

Several minutes later, Thomas rejoined the men at the table.

"So where were we?" he asked as if there wasn't an elephant in the room.

Marcus shook his head, chuckling. "You sure have a way with women, Tommy. I should have taken notes."

"Go to hell," Thomas snarled, "and if you call me 'Tommy' again, I'll kick your ass."

Another deep chuckle rumbled from Marcus. "You're in so deep, you can't even see daylight."

"Enough, Marcus," Cade ordered, then he looked at his stepson. "You can pretend your reactions to Julia and the mating aren't happening, but like I said, we'll talk about it when this meeting is over." Cade held up his hands when Thomas looked like he was going to blast him. "Don't get me wrong. Believe me, I get it. You have the same baffled expression each of us wore when we first met our mates. Women are confusing as hell."

THOMAS: Le Beau Series

Thomas glared at Cade for a moment longer and then gave him a single nod.

Simon grasped Thomas's forearm in solidarity. "If you ever want to talk, I'm here for you, as well."

He nodded again. "Okay. But I'm good." At least he hoped he was.

The security meeting seemed to take all day, when, in fact, it was only a half hour. As the men adjourned and stood to leave, Cade caught Thomas's attention.

"I would like you to come by the house and have a chat with your mother and me."

"I really don't think..."

"It wasn't a request."

Thomas narrowed his eyes on Cade, but in the end walked with him to the house his mother shared with his stepfather.

"Take a seat, son. Would you like anything to drink?"

"No, I'm good. Is this going to take long? I have things to do."

"Thomas!" Anna exclaimed as she walked through the front door.

"Hi, Mom."

Cade joined them carrying two cups of coffee. He kissed Anna on the cheek and handed a cup of decaf to her as he passed. "Cher, do you have a few minutes to chat with us?"

"Sure, what about?"

"Cade is butting in," Thomas groused.

"Thomas needs a come to Jesus lecture about mates," Cade corrected.

"Oh, I see." Anna nodded all too knowing.

"Can't you all just back off? I don't do

relationships." He turned to his mother, a tragic expression darkening his eyes. "Mom, you know I don't and why."

"Yes. I do, on both counts. I'm sorry I made such a horribly poor choice with my first husband. But, honey, a mate is something entirely different. You can't compare dating and a human relationship to that of a mate."

"Yeah, yeah. That's what you all say."

Cade looked at him. "There's a reason we all say it. It's true. Look at Simon and the way he suffered when he tried to let Rose go for her own good. Or Stefan and his nearly suicidal reaction to El's rejection. You can't throw away a blessed union the Goddess has set in motion. The ramifications are unspeakable."

Anna nodded in agreement to everything Cade said. It was all true, and Thomas knew that. He just didn't want it to be true for him.

"I hear what you're saying, and I'll get to know her and see where it goes. But – and this is a big – but. If you and the guys don't back off and leave us to figure this out, I'll end it right now.

Cade put up his hands in surrender. "I'll stay out of it. I only wanted this one talk. From here it's up to you."

"Baby, if you want any advice or if you have shifter relationship questions, please come to us and ask anything. Promise me you will talk to us and keep an open mind about the mating."

"I promise, Mom."

Thomas stood; he'd had enough touchy-feely for the day. As he made his way to the door, Anna grabbed him into a tight hug. Holding on like her life depended on it.

"It's okay, Mom. I promise."

THOMAS: Le Beau Series

"I love you, Thomas. With all my heart."

"I know. I love you, too."

Cade clapped him on the shoulder and gave him a thumbs-up as he walked out the door. At least that humiliation was over and done with.

Thank God they didn't know he had a date with Julia tonight or who knew how long he would've been trapped in a conversation from hell. He shivered to imagine what advice they would have given him.

A wave of excited fluttering erupted in his stomach. Just the thought of seeing Julia in a few hours had his pulse racing.

Lucas caught up to Thomas as he reached the main house. Now that the men had reviewed the security issues, he had a meeting with Grandpa.

"What did I miss? How did it go with Julia? Everything cool again?" Lucas shot questions at him at the speed of light.

"Yeah. As a matter of fact, I'm seeing her tonight at The Backwater," Thomas stated with a goofy smile on his lips.

Lucas clapped him on the back. "Sorry for messing with you. I couldn't help myself. But, man, you make it way too easy."

"You need to stay away from Stefan," Thomas grumbled. "He's wearing off on you and it's not attractive."

"That might be difficult seeing as we're both going to The Backwater tonight, too."

"Oh. Hell, no!"

"Don't worry." Lucas grinned. "We'll stay at the other end of the bar and pretend we don't know you."

"That's it." Thomas checked his gun and verified

the tie down was secure in his shoulder holster. "I need to leave."

Now Lucas frowned. "What for?"

"If I don't," Thomas glared at him, "I'm bound to shoot your ass," he said and stalked off.

Isaac walked into the living room where Lucas and Thomas were supposed to meet him.

"Is Thomas running late?" Isaac asked.

Lucas rubbed his neck sheepishly. "Not exactly."

"What is he – exactly?" Isaac growled. "What did you do?"

"I might have teased him a little bit and implied I was setting Julia up with one of my friends. And then told him we were going to be hanging out at The Backwater tonight when he is waiting for Julia to get off work."

"Dammit! We need to go over security procedures before any further social engagements. Which, now that I'm king again will be often. Fix this."

Isaac stomped out of the room shaking his head and mumbling about adolescence and stupidity.

*****

Julia hopped on one foot as she pulled on the tailored pants she was wearing tonight. Thomas would be here, and she wanted to wear something nicer than her normal blue jeans and t–shirt.

Now, for the hair. No amount of brushing, curling iron, or hair spray was going to force her hair into submission. GAH! She hated when the dreaded bad hair day snuck up on her, and she suddenly needed a salon appointment, like yesterday. A ponytail would look too little girlish. Tapping her chin she considered her options. That's when she remembered the hair clips in the back of the vanity drawer with her makeup.

A few hairstyle attempts later, and she was satisfied.

A touch of mascara and lip–gloss and she was set. If she did anything more, her oldest brother, Logan, who worked at the bar with her, would be suspicious, and the interrogation would begin.

She was just wiping down the last table when Logan came through the door.

"You look extra nice today, what's the occasion?"

Crud. Apparently she'd done too much.

"Can you keep a secret?"

That stopped Logan short. Narrowing his eyes at his little sister he growled, "What secret?"

"Oh stop. It's nothing bad. Actually, it's really good."

He folded his arms and continued to glare.

"For crying out loud." She sighed. "Keep it up and your face will freeze that way."

Logan didn't budge or look away.

"Fine. I found my mate at the gathering last night, and he is coming here tonight and then taking me out on a date."

Logan's eyes grew large, and his jaw dropped. "When? We didn't see you with anyone."

"After you went home."

"Who? Better not be that scrawny Jensen kid."

Julia laughed at his pained expression. "My mate is Thomas James, Cade's stepson. You know, the head of security."

"Oh, yeah, he's a good man." Logan wrapped her in a tight hug. "Congrats. Wish I could have found mine."

"Thank you, and you will when it's the right time."

"Think you could speed up the clock? I'm tired of checking out women and having meaningless relationships."

Julia patted his arm, "Maybe at the next social. I heard now that the king is in power again; there will be more social get–togethers. Thomas said he was going to be very busy ensuring Uncle Isaac's safety."

"As long as he has enough time for you," Logan said with concern in his eyes.

"It'll be fine."

"You say he's coming here?"

"Yep, later, closer to the end of my shift."

"I better call Dad and Quin."

"Whatever for?"

"The men of the family need to check this guy out."

She rolled her eyes. "Stay away from my mate and leave my relationship to me. I don't want any of you interfering."

Logan cracked his knuckles and acted tough. "When have I ever interfered?"

"Where should I begin?" She laughed.

"Okay...okay." He raised his hands in surrender. "I'll just quietly keep an eye on him and I promise to stay out of the way."

Julia stood on tiptoes and kissed his cheek. "Thank you. Now, let's get to work and prep the bar."

A while later, she leaned against the bar daydreaming about Thomas. Tall, but not too tall, broad shoulders, and muscles in perfect proportion for his fit body. Her pulse began to race, visualizing him. Ducking her head, she hid behind a curtain of hair before Logan saw the deep red rise up her neck. Just thinking of Tommy set her body on fire.

THOMAS: Le Beau Series

"Hey, sis, I could use some help over here."

Logan was trying to install a new daiquiri and margarita machine. The man loved his gadgets.

She forced herself to take a deep, steadying breath before stepping away from the edge of the bar. "What do you need me to do?"

"Just hold that level while I attach this."

Logan was a genius with all things mechanical and could build anything by simply looking at it. Finally, a man who could put something together correctly without extra parts left over while never opening the instruction manual.

A few screws in place and he stepped back. "Okay, you can let go and hit the power button."

The frozen drink maker came to life, auger blade turning and ready for the drink mix.

"I know quite a few people who will be very excited about this," Julia said, grinning. "Have I told you lately how amazing you are?"

Logan shook his head grinning as he wiped his hands on a bar towel. "Not yet today."

"Well, you are. You'll make some woman a wonderful mate one day. I hope it's very soon, too."

"Thanks," Logan said, turning a slight shade of pink. He never could take compliments without embarrassment.

*****

The day had crept by. The dinner rush was already in full swing, and Thomas still hadn't arrived. Every time the door opened, her gaze shot to see if it was him. Maybe he wasn't coming after all.

V.A. Dold

She turned away from a large group filing through the door. Thomas would be coming alone so no need to search that crowd. With a sad sigh, she went back to the drink she was mixing.

Seconds later, the hair stood on the back of her neck in awareness, and her wolf lifted her head to sniff the air.

What the heck?

Julia glanced around the bar, and there he was, alone at a table, staring at her. Her breath caught in her throat. How could he become more handsome in the last few hours? Thomas was the most extraordinary representation of male physiology she had ever laid eyes on.

He wore his hair a little longer than most would expect of his position, after all, he was a very powerful man as the head of security for Uncle Isaac. But, she admitted as she grinned to herself, she liked it. His dark mane looked slightly tussled tonight. If she didn't know he was the sheriff, so to speak, he'd look one hundred percent bad boy. It wasn't hard to picture him on a Harley speeding down the highway.

His blue eyes, though soft and sweet when he looked at her, could turn lethal before you blinked when he was on duty. The contrast of those eyes and his tanned skin had her absolutely hypnotized, and now had her mouth watering. Quickly she dabbed the corners for drool. Thank Goddess for small favors, she hadn't made a fool of herself yet, but she still had all night, so she knocked on the wooden bar top.

There was something very wild and masculine about the casual way he sat at his table drinking her in. Slowly, his gaze traveled from her eyes to her mouth. As his stare became more intense, he licked his lips, and she almost dropped to the floor. Her heart pounded, and knees went weak. She had no idea how she was going to make it through her shift.

"Something wrong?"

Startled, she jumped, and then, like an idiot, stood blinking at Logan, who was watching her very closely.

"No. What would possibly be wrong?"

Logan frowned at her skeptically. "You have a dazed kind of expression that I've never seen before." Before she could bat his hand away, he felt her forehead for a fever. "Are you feeling all right?"

She leaned away and growled at him. "Hey, keep your hands to yourself, buddy."

Thomas seemed to be keeping his distance and allowing her to work her shift without distraction. That was laughable; his being in the building was all it took to distract her. Logan made worried noises behind her as she messed up yet another drink order.

"Oh, shut up and mind your own business."

"I'm really concerned, sis. You never screw up like you are tonight. Want to tell me what's going on?"

"No."

"That's it? No?"

"Exactly. I'm fine, and I don't want to talk about it."

Logan eyed her again, shook his head, and took the next order.

*****

"Thomas?"

Thomas went ridged as a provocative purr he knew all too well whispered next to his ear, and arms draped across his chest from behind. Lori. Average, curvy, and stacked with double Ds, she once aroused his lust.

That is until Julia opened his eyes.

Thomas let out a long, exasperated breath; he really didn't want to cause a scene. And he especially didn't want Julia to see Lori hanging all over him. He grimaced as she massaged his chest and shot a worried glance toward the bar.

Before he could peel her off, she said much too loudly, "I want you so bad, baby. Let's get out of here."

Ah. Hell, no!

A hard jerk dislodged her claws from his shirt, leaving a small tear behind. Hopefully, no one would notice, primarily, a certain bartender or her now glowering brother.

SHIT!

Lori rubbed her wrist where Thomas grabbed her. Thomas learned a second too late that she still hadn't gotten the hint; apparently she was thinking he was playing rough or something. A fire lit in her eyes right before she shoved her hand into his pants and grabbed his cock. Then, to seal his fate, Lori rubbed her cleavage against his face.

"Get the hell off me!" Thomas barked a bit louder than he intended as he launched himself from his seat.

Lori looked stunned by his outburst, but slowly the surprise turned dark. "You aren't mated, are you?"

That would be the natural assumption of a woman as self–absorbed as Lori was. Of course, there could be no other reason for a man to reject her as far as she was concerned.

Like a snake striking, she pulled the collar of his shirt open, looking for the mating mark.

THOMAS: Le Beau Series

Yanking his collar from her grip he spat, "Yes, I've found a mate, and it isn't you, thank God."

Lori looked like he'd slapped her, then leaned closer to hiss, "In your dreams, little man. My mate will have more to offer down," her gaze trailed to his crotch, "there."

With an evil smile, she flipped her hair over her shoulder and sauntered to another table. Poor guy, he hoped the man knew what he was getting into.

With more composure than he was feeling, Thomas gave a nod to the patrons eyeing him and sat at his table once more. Afraid to look toward Julia, he focused on his beer.

His heart was almost beating normally again when a large hand slammed down on his tabletop. Lucky for the man attached to that arm, he wasn't packing. Instantly, his sheriff persona was in place.

Any man or shifter with a lick of sense would have backed off. But not Logan, at least not when the situation involved one of his sisters. He was getting an explanation, and it was happening right here, right now.

"You'd better start talking, asshole. Your stench is all over my sister, and she told me she found her mate last night. I'm assuming that man is you," Logan snarled. "So, the question is, if you're Julia's mate, why are you letting Lori shove her hand down your pants?"

Thomas knew better than to fight with one of Julia's brothers. She wouldn't thank him for that. Instead, he put his hands up in surrender and waved Logan to join him at the table.

"First off, yes, I'm Julia's mate. Second, I dated Lori, once. I didn't encourage her tonight in any way and the instant she got handsy I put an end to it." Then

V.A. Dold

Thomas glared at Logan. "Perhaps you missed the part where I told her I had indeed found my mate? Or the part where I told her to get off me?"

Logan clapped Thomas on the back and grinned in satisfaction. "Good answer. Welcome to the family."

"Thanks." Thomas sighed in relief. Then he frowned. "I had no idea Lori was a shifter."

"She's not, she's human. Her sister is a mate, and ever since she found out, she's been trolling for one of her own. I pity the man who gets saddled with that one."

As if they had been discussing the weather, Logan walked back to his station behind the bar like nothing had happened.

Shifters are nuts.

But, as he considered the crazy world he was now fully a part of, his thoughts turned to Julia. The way she'd looked as she danced with him. Her lips kiss–swollen and her eyes begging him for more. Bingo. He was hard as a rock. A quick adjustment and he was a little more comfortable, but not much.

He wasn't a coward by any means, but the thought of seeing a look of disappointment or hurt on Julia's face had his gut in knots. Gathering his courage, he looked her straight in the eye. His heart lurched – she looked lost and hurt.

Sad.

Immediate action was required. Thomas pushed back from the table and made a beeline to Julia. Without asking permission, he walked behind the bar, took Julia's hand and caught Logan's eye.

"We need a minute."

THOMAS: Le Beau Series

He didn't bother to wait for a response, experience with shifters had taught him, when it came to mates, everything else was secondary, even work.

"Where's your office?"

She nodded toward the far corner. "Over there."

Once the door was shut, Thomas took Julia's face in his hands.

"Baby, what did you see?"

She wouldn't look at him and when she attempted to answer only a whimper came out.

"Sweetheart, that woman is someone I dated once and only once. I have zero interest in her, and if you were listening I'm sure you heard me tell her that."

Julia nodded but still didn't look at him. Finally, she spoke. "I saw her," she hiccupped, "caress you and stick her hand..." a sob broke from her throat.

"Did you also see me jump away from her and yell at her to get off of me?"

She nodded.

"So, can you tell me what the problem is?"

She hesitated. How do you tell your mate you suddenly feel inadequate?

He had no idea how, but he felt her anxiety and pain, and the only thing he could think to do was kiss her all better. Slowly, he leaned closer.

Julia wet her lips, which caused Thomas to inhale sharply when he felt her tongue flick across his lower lip. That deep breath took in her fresh snow scent and muddled all his senses. Fighting this attraction was downright stupid, and he had no intention of being stupid. No, his intention was just the opposite.

His desire pounded through his veins until he vibrated with it. Cupping her face, he captured her lips with his own. Excitement and desire tightened Thomas's gut and forced a tortured groan from his throat that rumbled in the room. Thomas devoured her mouth like a starved man.

A soft moan rose from her lips as she kissed him back just as passionately. His fingers tangled in her hair; then he angled her head perfectly to deepen the kiss further. He swore he heard the click of puzzle pieces snapping together, and he was lost.

Her hands slid around his neck to pull him closer, the fit of their bodies was perfection and the press of her breasts into his chest drove him wild. The feel and scent of her pushed his desire higher. He craved her touch, her companionship, her love.

The friction of hips grinding against hips brought him to the edge of release. His rock hard erection was pressed against her belly straining for liberation from his jeans. But he knew, without a doubt, a quickie was out of the question and would never be enough to satisfy either of them. When he made love to Julia, he wanted the entire night to pleasure her and explore her body, not a tawdry few minutes in a public place. Damning the fact they were in her office with a hundred shifters on the other side of the door, not to mention her brother who would kick his ass, he slowed the kiss. She moaned softly into his mouth while his tongue danced with hers one last time.

It took all his resolve to lift his lips from hers and open his eyes. Pressing his forehead to hers, only the sound of their ragged breathing broke the silence. The hurt that had occupied her expression before was now replaced with passion and longing.

THOMAS: Le Beau Series

Every breath brushed her pebble hard nipples against his chest. A shudder racked his body as he fought for control. He had to get them out of her office and put at least a sliver of daylight between them. Otherwise his resolve wasn't going to be enough.

Chapter 6

Thomas's finger combed his hair as he watched Julia straighten her clothes before checking her hair and makeup. He was relieved when she finished, and she looked like they had simply been having a conversation. The last thing he needed was Logan launching him out the door for molesting his sister.

As he held the office door open for Julia, he glanced over her head toward the bar. Logan watched them closely and gave him an approving nod when he saw his sister's smile.

Chuckling under his breath, he shook his head. *Shifters are strange.*

A human would kill another guy for messing with his sister, but shifters were all good with it as long as you made the woman happy and respected her.

Julia took her place behind the bar without so much as a glance at her brother while Thomas found an open table. There was still a bit of time before she finished her shift, so he got comfortable. Not more than ten minutes later Stefan, Lucas, and Marcus joined him. El was speaking at a university tonight, which left Stefan with free time on his hands. As far as he was concerned, as long as they behaved themselves, he was happy to see them.

An hour later Julia was cleaning her end of the bar and preparing to clock out. As she walked from behind the serving area, she had two bags of garbage in her hands. No man worth his salt would allow his woman to struggle under a load like that. He was at her side in an instant, relieving her of the bags.

"I've got those. Let me take these out while you finish up."

Stefan watched Thomas head for the garbage bin behind the building. A disturbance among the wild creatures caught his attention. Something wasn't right, and whatever it was had the wildlife upset.

Quickly he asked the birds what they could see. The image of half a dozen shifters circling a single man popped into his head. Thomas was about to be handed a shit storm of trouble and a world of hurt.

Julia was busy making a monster order of drinks when she heard Thomas cursing in her mind and received a flurry of scrambled images.

The backyard.

Men all around.

Fists flying.

Tommy!

Stay...inside.

Frantically, she looked at her brother and then her cousins. She didn't need to say a word. All the men were already headed for the door.

She bellowed what could only be described as a war cry and cleared the bar in one powerful leap.

V.A. Dold

Mess with my mate and you answer to me, boys.

She was right on the men's heels as they rounded the corner of the bar and headed for the dumpster. Just like the flashes she'd received from her mate, a gang of shifters surrounded Thomas. It was one of the swamp packs. Wolves who rarely surfaced and lived like it was nineteen hundred instead of twenty fifteen, and most of them considered humans second-class. Which was asinine and why the majority of the men had no mate. Idiots. The human population was where ninety-five percent of the mates came from.

Julia recognized the ringleader, Blade. He'd been causing trouble since he cut teeth. After a bar fight that he'd started trashed her bar, he had been banned from The Backwater for life. Every decent male she knew hated that punk and was looking for the opportunity to take a bite out of him.

The moron had been hitting on her for decades even though he knew everything about him chafed her ass. The idiot didn't seem to understand the word no. More than once she'd wondered if his stupidity was a product of his shallow gene pool. The Goddess must really have it in for the swampers, the last mating she had heard about was between cousins. No wonder they were so inbred.

His dunce squad was always looking for a fight. Her belief was their insanity stemmed from a lack of sex, their lack any way. No decent woman would let them near her. Sexual frustration was her theory to explain their inexcusable aggressive behavior, and she was sticking to that theory.

Thomas had taken two of them down before they got hold of him. Both lay writhing at his feet, as he stood pinned between two others while a third used him as a punching bag.

He was trying to free himself to fight back, but he was held tight, covered in bruises, and blood flowed steadily from his nose and mouth.

Fury spread like a thick red haze over her vision as she launched a hailstorm of empty liquor bottles from the dumpster, at the goon squad's heads. Her enraged roar and the flying bottles stopped the rescue party in their tracks. There were so many heavy glass bottles in the air; they had no way to reach Thomas without being knocked senseless.

Arms thrown wide, she drew every loose object within two hundred feet to her and directed all of it at Blade and his minions. After over one hundred years of practice, her accuracy and aim were unprecedented. Not a single missile struck Thomas, even though he was in the center of the hailstorm. Cries and howls of pain from the cowering swampers filled the air as more people filed into the yard from the bar.

Logan tentatively tapped Julia on the shoulder. "As much as I'm enjoying the show, we need to get to Thomas."

Julia nodded once and allowed all the objects flying to fall harmlessly to the ground. All that is, except one. A rather large, heavy lead pipe from the plumbing renovations she had just completed slammed into Blade's crotch before it joined the bottles and branches to lie silently around the bloodied swamp rats. Blade's scream of pain made every man's ears within two miles bleed.

Before Logan or her cousins could move, the dunce squad shifted and darted for the deep swamp. A group of men from the bar shifted to chase them down, but Julia

V.A. Dold

knew they would never find them. They were already scattered like schoolyard bullies, and no doubt hiding in one of their secret holes no one else was ever able to locate. In the deep bayou, they easily became invisible, using their ability to run and hide to survive.

"Damn, Julia," Stefan said in awe.

"You ruined all our fun," Marcus and Lucas griped.

"Momma is going to have a cow." Logan shook his head. "You know how she feels about you using your telekinesis gift."

"So don't tell her," Julia panted. "Now come over here and help me get him into my house."

Julia lived in a two–bedroom cottage she had built on the land behind the bar. It wasn't a palace, but it was comfortable and convenient for her with the bar next door.

Marcus and Lucas helped Thomas up, and each wrapped an arm around him to help him walk the short distance.

Glancing over her shoulder at Logan, Julia asked, "Would you make sure the bar gets closed on time?"

"You got it. Let me know how he is."

If left up to the local shifters, The Backwater would be rocking twenty–four seven. Someone needed to shoo them out at closing time, and she had her hands full at the moment.

"Can you lay him on the couch? I'll get the med kit and a washcloth from the bathroom."

"You got it."

Thomas groaned as he was lowered to the cushions. "I feel like I was hit by a bus, then it backed up to make sure it finished the job."

THOMAS: Le Beau Series

Marcus was very quiet; Stefan knew he was concerned about injuries they weren't seeing. Those shifters looked like they were trying to turn his ribs into dust, and there were sure to be a few broken or cracked.

"Julia, I think I should call Anna and the healers," Stefan called toward the hallway she had just walked down.

"I was thinking the same thing. I suck at healing, and I think he's going to need them."

Stefan pulled out his cell phone while Marcus took a seat across the room, and Lucas stood in the doorframe. A steady stream of growls rumbled from Marcus's chest, as he stared out a window at the swamp.

Seconds later, Julia hustled into the room with arms loaded. "First, we need to clean you up so I can see how bad your cuts are." She needed to keep talking and concentrate on the task at hand, or the tears she held in check would flow.

"The other healers are unavailable, but Anna and Mom are on their way, as well as Cade and Dad," Stefan said as he shoved the phone in his pocket. "Dad wants a report about what happened, and he wasn't about to let the women come here unescorted."

"When are Jack and Michael joining the guard?" Marcus snarled.

"I'm meeting with Etienne and the guys in a couple days," Thomas hissed, as Julia dabbed around his left eye.

Lucas narrowed his gaze on his brother. "What are you planning, Marcus?"

"Vampire senses will come in handy," Marcus growled as he turned away from the window, "when I go swamper hunting."

V.A. Dold

"Excellent idea. The moment they laid a hand on Thomas they signed their own death warrants," Stefan growled.

Twenty minutes later Stefan cocked his head. "I hear Mom and Dad coming to the door."

Julia met them at the door before they could knock. "Hello, everyone."

"How are you, cher?" Emma asked as she drew her in for a tight hug. Then Isaac hugged her gently as Cade smiled hello.

"I'm good, but Thomas has had better days. Please, come in. He's on the couch through there."

"Don't worry, cher. Thomas will be fine," Anna said as she gave her a quick hug.

"Hi, Grandma. Hey, Mom," Thomas said as he tried to smile through the pain.

"Oh, cher. What did those animals do to you?" Emma cried.

Anna gasped and rushed to hold him in her arms, but she instead stood frowning and seemed afraid to touch him. Finally, a whimper escaped her quivering lips before she could suppress it.

When Emma stepped to the end of the couch, Isaac got his first look at Thomas's face. Furious energy flooded the room as everyone heard vicious snarls in their minds.

Mon amour. You're sending telepathy to everyone.

Julia frowned at Thomas. "Why are you growling at your grandfather?"

His eyes grew wide in surprise. "Wasn't me."

They looked at each other for a heartbeat, then glanced around the room.

THOMAS: Le Beau Series

Everyone gaped at Isaac as he slowly raised his hand. "It was me."

"What the hell, Dad?" Stefan, Lucas, and Marcus yelled together.

"Except for Cade, you're all too young to remember, but as king, I had a few special things I could do. Talking telepathically to all shifters under my rule was one of them."

"So..." Marcus hedged. "Can we answer you?"

"Yes, you can. Now, anyway. Triggering the ability required two things, I had to be the ruling king, which I am again, and I had to initiate telepathic communication. Which, apparently, I just did. When you were children, and I gave up the throne, I lost that ability," he shrugged. "It looks like it's back."

Stefan and Marcus sat back in their chairs, flabbergasted. Their reaction was rare, very little affected the brothers the way this bombshell had.

"Well," Emma said to break the silence. "Should we get busy, Anna?"

"Oh. Yes," Anna said, shaking off her own surprised stupor.

Repositioning, Anna sat near Thomas's head as Emma sat at his feet.

"Since there are only the two of us, we'll send healing energy through you from opposite ends. The Goddess will guide the energy where it is needed," Emma explained as she wrapped her fingers around his ankles.

Julia was enthralled; the healers were incredible to watch. Before her eyes, the swelling of Thomas's left eye went down, and the bruising faded. As she strained to listen, his breathing became smoother, and there was a pronounced reduction in the rattle she had heard in his lungs earlier. Before they ended the session, his lips returned to normal, the swelling and split skin gone.

Finally, Emma stood. Julia thought she was done, but instead she moved to join Anna by his head. A concerned expression creased her brow as her hands hovered over his forehead and then around the sides of his skull. She didn't actually touch Thomas; rather, it looked like she was sensing something.

"Are you sensing what I feel?" Anna asked.

"I believe there's a fracture along the left side running from above his ear to the eye socket."

"That's where I was feeling an injury as well," Anna agreed.

Isaac, my love, we need a little help. Please have everyone send as much energy as possible to Thomas.

"Ladies and gentlemen, we need to lend a little assistance. Hold your palm out toward Thomas and imagine a door opening at the top of your head to allow the Goddess to funnel energy through you and out your palm. In your mind, see the energy flowing to Thomas."

The room was silent for a very long ten minutes before Emma spoke. "That should do it. Are you sensing anything else, Anna?"

There was a moment's pause before she shook her head. "I think we've done all we can."

Thomas sat up and rubbed his head as if testing it out. "Wow, I feel a lot better." He smiled at his mother and grandmother as he hugged them. "Thank you."

"You're welcome, cher," Emma beamed.

Anna swatted his arm. "Don't you ever scare me like that again." Then she pulled him in for a second hug.

THOMAS: Le Beau Series

"Geez, Mom. It wasn't like I picked a bar fight. I was just taking out the trash, and those goons jumped me."

"Are you feeling well enough to tell us what happened?" Cade asked.

"I offered to take out the trash while Julia finished up at the bar. I didn't realize they were there until the first one jumped me from behind. They must have been laying in wait..."

That's when it occurred to him...

"Babe, do you always take out the trash, or is that job shared between all the employees?"

She let out a snort at the idea Logan would lower himself to trash duty. "I do it."

"Hell, no!" Lucas barked. "No one assaults our women."

Julia looked confused. "I wasn't the one attacked."

"No, babe, but you were the one they expected. So, it stands to reason; you were the target."

"Oh. I see."

Isaac leaned forward. "Do you remember anything they said?"

"One thing was more than evident," Thomas said as he took Julia's hand. "They hate humans mating with shifters."

Isaac nodded. "That's been a long-held sentiment amongst the swamp shifters."

Cade watched as Thomas snuggled Julia under his arm on the couch.

Grinning, he stood and helped Anna with her coat. "I think our work here is done." Then his expression became serious. "Cher, I don't like the idea of you taking out the trash alone for a while and I would prefer you didn't open or close the bar alone either," Cade suggested.

"I agree. It's not safe, babe," Thomas said as he caressed the soft skin of her inner wrist. "If Logan can't be with you, call me. Either I or one of the guards, will be more than happy to help you open and close."

She opened her mouth to object, but Thomas put a finger across her lips. "I need to know you're safe. Please, humor me."

Blushing, she nodded. "If it makes you feel better, I'll do my best to not be alone at the bar or outside in the back."

Isaac was helping Emma into her coat and gave a pointed look to his sons.

"We should head home," Stefan said, getting to his feet.

"Yeah, I have things to do, too," Marcus added.

"Oh, yeah. What they said." Lucas grinned.

After they were gone, Julia covered her mouth and giggled. "They couldn't have been any more obvious, could they?"

Thomas shook his head and laughed, "At least they're gone." Then, he pulled her in for a kiss.

"Tommy," Julia drew back, "I think you need a shower."

"What?" And then he noticed how bloody his shirt was. "Did I get some on you?"

Worried he had ruined her shirt, he scooted back to check the damage.

"Just a little. It's okay, a little cold water and it will come right out. I have a robe you can use while I give your clothes a quick wash. Would you like me to get it for you?"

"Yes, thank you. Otherwise, once this dries, my shirt is going to be stiff and crunchy."

"Ewww." Julia scrunched her nose and laughed.

"By the way, I kind of like you calling me Tommy."

"It's the way I think of you, but if you're just being polite, I'll call you Thomas like everyone else."

Thomas considered that for a minute. "No, I like it. But no one else better try calling me that. Only you have that privilege." He stood and held out his hand to her, then let her lead the way.

The laundry was washing, and Tommy was in the shower, now she could relax for a minute. Julia settled back on the couch smiling and put her fingers to her lips. She could still taste Thomas, and she relished it. She'd never had a man kiss her the way he did. It was sinful and wicked and, oh, so wonderful.

Suddenly Lucinda's face popped into her mind with a sour disapproving expression. She could already hear her mother screaming that Thomas was below her and unacceptable as her mate. Then she would start in on how he wasn't the right kind of man for her and only a security guard. Her mother was going to have a seizure when she found out she'd kissed; never mind was mated to, a man as lowly as Thomas.

But that didn't matter to her. Thomas was perfect and by no means lowly. Why her mother couldn't see the power he held not only in his position as head of security, but also in the gift he would receive when they completed the ritual, she had no idea.

*****

Ten minutes later, Thomas walked toward Julia, looking sexy as sin; towel slung low on his hips, robe hanging open, and hair damp and messy from the towel dry he'd given it.

"Sorry about the lack of fashion, babe. How long until my clothes are dry?"

Julia's eyes grew heated as she took him in from head to very bare toes. "Clothes? Who needs clothes?"

Before Thomas could respond, a flash of night running lights from a boat caught his eye through the window. "You have a visitor."

Julia looked toward the window frowning. No one should be at her house. It was late, and she was supposed to be on a date.

Mother?

Julia heaved an exasperated breath as she rolled her eyes at him. "Let me handle her."

Thomas looked toward the window suspiciously. "Are you sure?"

She nodded. Her mother irritated him; she felt it immediately at the gathering. Hell, she irritated everyone, and knowing her mother's propensity for dramatics and outbursts, she didn't want Tommy to do or say anything he might regret. Not that she cared what he said to her mother, but Tommy might, and she didn't want him to feel bad about it later.

With a single nod to show his agreement with her decision, he adjusted his robe as best he could as the deadbolt rattled mere heartbeats before Lucinda stormed into Julia's living room. Her hair was flying willy–nilly around her shoulders as if it was alive, and rage colored her face a truly unique shade of red.

"What on earth are you thinking, young lady!"

"That I would like pasta for dinner?" Julia quipped

THOMAS: Le Beau Series

"You know darn well, I'm not talking about dinner. You used your gift tonight and made a spectacle of yourself."

"Yes, I certainly did." Julia let out a long, exasperated breath. Then her eyes narrowed on Lucinda. How did she know she'd used her gift? "There were a few swampers who needed to learn a lesson."

Her mother snarled angrily at her reply, and then sniffed, wrinkling her nose like she smelled a skunk. As if Thomas wasn't standing right in front of her. "Human. Why is there a filthy human in my house?"

"Because I invited him into 'MY' house," she growled back, rubbing at the sudden pain she felt behind her eyes. "Do you mind if I take a look at your house key?"

Her mother frowned at her odd question but handed her the key anyway.

Without a word, Julia walked to the bathroom and flushed the key down the toilet.

"What the hell did you do that for?" Lucinda shrieked.

"Is this house on the land owned by the bar?"

"You know it is. Now, why did you do that?"

"Is the bar solely in my name?"

"Of course it is. And, again, you know that. What's this about?"

"You are no longer allowed to barge into 'My' home uninvited, nor are you allowed to show up whenever you want to. You will call first and ask permission to come over or wait for an invitation. Then, and only then, will you be allowed into this house."

"I will do whatever I please. I paid for this house and that bar."

V.A. Dold

"Where the money came from matters little, whose name is on the deed is what's important. You have no power or voice here on my property. Now, leave before I call the bouncer from the bar and have you forcibly removed."

Chapter 7

Her mother glared at her. "Don't get smart with me, young lady. I'm sure you don't want your father to know the way you talk to me."

"Ah, Mother. See, there you're wrong. Go ahead and tell him. Then when he asks me why, I'll fill him in on how you hate humans. Oh, and how you've been shopping both Krystal and me around to every pack in the state. What do you think he'll say about 'your' behavior?"

Her mother curled her lip as she eyed Thomas, acknowledging him for the first time. "And what is that you have on, Thomas?" Lucinda virtually spat his name like a dirty word. "Don't you possess clothes of your own?"

Cocking an eyebrow, he glanced down at the robe. He hardly looked like a homeless person; she was simply being vicious, and he knew it. Her nasty attitude made it imperative he mess with her.

"Haven't you heard? Freshly showered is the latest thing in fashion." He gave Lucinda a wicked grin and widened the gap in the robe across his chest to show a little more flesh. "Besides, Julia thinks I'm sexy dressed like this." For added measure, he waggled his eyebrows at her.

"With that outfit and attitude," she looked him up and down then sneered, "you should be working a corner somewhere."

Thomas rubbed his chin and nodded thoughtfully. "That might be true, but the question is, 'MOM'," he turned left and then right to allow her a complete appraisal, "do I look like a cut–rate prostitute or a high–end escort?" Thomas emphasized the fact that he referred to her as his mother to rub her nose in a situation he knew she detested.

"You sure don't look like a hooker to me," Julia purred as she wrapped an arm around his waist. "You look HOT!"

He smiled at her and gave her a playful whisker rub across her cheek as she giggled and wriggled away.

Her mother growled at their cozy behavior.

"Give it a rest, Mother. He's my mate and," she kissed him solidly on the lips to emphasize her point, "I'm rapidly falling in love with him."

Lucinda took a menacing step further into the room, and Julia felt Tommy adjust his stance as if he was preparing to fight her.

Glancing up at him, she patted his chest affectionately. "I got this, cher."

Thomas relented but remained on the ready, glaring his own challenge at his soon to be mother–in–law. She made one threatening move and, mother–in–law or not, he would take her down.

THOMAS: Le Beau Series

"Were you hit on the head during your little bar fight?" Lucinda hissed. "You can't mate...that," she spat as she shook a finger at Thomas.

"Mother, I'm only going to say this once, so listen up. Your opinion means nothing to us. This is my life, not yours, and I'm living it without your interference. If you would like to be a part of it, mind your own business and keep your opinions to yourself. If not, that's fine, too."

Her mother's beautiful face turned stony with suppressed fury. "No. You listen up. That bar doesn't even come close to producing enough money to pay your bills. As it stands, I pay more of your monthly budget than that den of iniquity provides. So, little girl, I essentially own you. You mate this human, and you're through. I'll cut you off so fast, you won't know what hit you."

"No problem," she said shrugging her shoulders. "I'll mate Tommy tonight and we can pool our incomes. I don't need your money or the strings attached to it."

Her mother looked like she was going to lose her lunch. "You can't live on his 'rent-a-cop' income."

"Now, there you're wrong again and horribly misinformed, Mother. Tommy can and will, easily support me."

Rage twisted Lucinda's expression. "How dare you defy me. And for what?" She spat on the floor at Thomas's feet. "A low-rent roll in the sack?"

"Now, that's just nasty, Mother. This is about me and Tommy, my mate. My love life has nothing to do with you."

She narrowed her eyes at Julia. "I'm cutting you off immediately."

V.A. Dold

"Okay."

"I'm not joking, Julia. I make one call, and you will know what it's like to be poor."

She snuggled deeper into Tommy's arms and turned slightly to speak over her shoulder.

"So where would you like to live, cher?"

Thomas grinned at her and tightened his hold. "Well, we have this house, but it's a bit far from Isaac. There's my brand new two–story, five–bedroom house on my family's plantation. Or, I could build us a new house half way between the two. Although the ten million dollars Isaac deposited into my account, last week may not build a house large enough for my lady. For you, only the best will do. Maybe I should take Isaac up on his offer and utilize the family account, that has billions in it and I have unlimited access to use any of it as I see fit."

Tapping his lips, he made a sucking noise with his teeth. "But you know, The Backwater is pretty far from the plantation and I hate the thought of you so far away from me. I think we should relocate the entire place closer to the royal compound and stay in my new house for a while until we make up our minds."

"You think we can lift the whole place and place it on new pilings?"

He nodded. "Yeah. I'll get my architect on it, and we should be able to move in by the end of the month."

Her mother's eyes were growing larger with each option. "Lies. All lies," she screamed.

"What lies, Mother?" Thomas frowned.

"He's lying to you, Julia. Why would Isaac give a human who isn't blood related to him in any way a cent. Heck, he's lucky Isaac gave him a job at all. And stop calling me 'Mother.'"

THOMAS: Le Beau Series

Thomas arched a brow at her mother. "I'm really beginning to think you don't like me. It's time for you to leave."

Thomas gave Julia a quick kiss before he stepped around her and grabbed Lucinda's arm.

Her eyes about bulged out of her head, and her jaw actually went slack. "Take your filthy hands off me!"

"See you around, Mother," Julia smiled and waved. "And say hi to Daddy for me."

It was the first time in her life she'd seen her mother tossed out of anywhere, and it felt great.

She took Tommy's hand as he closed the door on Lucinda's still shrieking face. He flipped the deadbolt as a giggle bubbled up from her throat.

"This must be what it feels like to be truly free."

He swung her around as they laughed like school children.

"You okay, babe? That was pretty harsh and intense."

"I'm perfect. I finally feel happy. Really happy. It's like a ton has been lifted from my shoulders, and if I'm not careful, I'll float away."

A new, uncharted future unfolded before her. No—before them. It was beautiful and filled with unlimited possibilities. And she was excited by the challenges and blessings ahead.

As they cuddled on the couch, she expected her phone to start ringing off the hook, but it remained silent. Apparently, her mother didn't want her father to know what she'd been up to. That was okay – for now.

Thomas tipped her chin to look into her eyes. "You sure you're okay?"

"Absolutely."

Thomas turned her hand up and kissed the center of her palm. "So, didn't we have a first date to enjoy?"

She gave him a saucy grin. "I vote we stay home and watch action movies instead. I'm all pumped up and could use a Die Hard marathon."

Thomas gave her an amused grin. "You're a Bruce fan? Now I know I'm in love."

"Remember that when I want to watch a chick flick."

As Thomas set up the movie, Julia made popcorn. She paused for a moment and sighed. As horrible as her mother could be, the little girl in her wanted her mother to change and be the loving parent she had been. She wasn't sure what had happened to change her mother, but about one hundred years ago she started to go a little crazy, and now she was straight up insane.

I wonder if the healers can cure crazy?

"Goodbye, Momma," she whispered to the empty kitchen.

She hoped one day her mother would be normal again, but she seriously worried it would never happen. The person she worried for the most was her father. They were mated, and if her mother died, he would, too. She wasn't sure she could take losing her father.

Walking into the living room, she smiled at Tommy. Thank Goddess for him.

He reached out and took the bowl filled with popcorn so she could snuggle up beside him. "The price for the movie is a kiss," he teased.

"I don't know; that's a pretty high price," she teased back.

Laughing, he pulled her in for a long kiss that would have steamed the windows of his car.

THOMAS: Le Beau Series

Leaning his forehead against hers, he caught his breath. "Okay, it's Die Hard time."

Twenty minutes into the movie Thomas was dying to talk about their mating relationship; they had both seen the movie multiple times so why not talk, too.

"You know what I smell whenever you come near me?"

Julia glanced away from the TV and grinned. "What?"

"Freshly fallen snow. A crisp winter day in Denver."

"Really?" Julia scrunched up her nose. "I've never even seen snow."

"You're kidding me."

"No. I've never left Louisiana."

"First thing we do once we're mated is go someplace with snow," Thomas declared. "That's just not right."

Julia laughed at his distraught expression. "I smell warm spices, like cinnamon and nutmeg, when you come near."

"Spicy," Thomas nodded with a manly satisfied grin. "I like spicy."

Julia gave him a playful swat on the arm. "Don't let it go to your head, he-man."

Thomas laughed and hugged her tighter to show just how strong and manly he was.

Were you able to sense me as your mate during the gathering, even though you're still human?

Thomas liked using telepathy. Now he appreciated and understood the intimacy of that way of communication.

V.A. Dold

I had a strong attraction to you and couldn't stop staring at you. And I caught your scent. He thought it through further. *And we can talk telepathically, so, yeah, I guess so.*

"No one else can smell your snowy perfume but me, right?" Thomas asked.

"Nope," Julia grinned. "That's reserved only for my mate."

"Did you have a strong reaction to my voice? Cade said when the male shifter heard his mate's voice; the effect is amazing. That your animal soul recognizes its other half."

"Yeah, I did. It was pretty shocking; I'm surprised it didn't knock me off my feet. But there's really no way to describe it. The effect certainly assured me I had found my mate. You're the only person who can complete me."

"I know from talking to my mom that the mating is more permanent than any human wedding can ever be. That being said, she still had a wedding, but Rose and Simon chose not to, and then Stefan and El kind of did a quick wedding at the gathering. What do you want to do?"

"It's true that a mate is like being married, and yet so much more. Since we were created to complete each other by each having the other's half of a soul, once the pieces are joined there's no separating that. I guess I need to think about the whole wedding thing. Until now I hadn't given it much thought."

"To tell the truth, neither have I. I never felt anything more than physical attraction for a woman before I met you. So, there was no reason to think about getting married. Is that because I was destined to be your mate? Did my half of the soul prevent me from getting too attached?"

"Maybe." Julia thought about it and then added. "I would bet it did."

"I'm really excited to be able to shift. Is the mating ritual the same for me? Or is it different when the man is human, and the woman is the shifter?"

"It's still the same except I will recite the words first since I'm the shifter. Have any of the guys described the claiming to you? I'm sure you understand being a mate and the combining of our souls, right?"

"Cade and mom explained a little when we first found out she was a shifter, but, needless to say, they didn't go into details. That would have been too many levels of wrong."

"As far as the ritual goes, when we do it, it's going to be a little backward. Usually, the man says the first part and the woman says the second, but, since I'm the shifter, I'll say the first part. There are several parts to the ritual."

"Hold that thought. Let me grab a pen and paper so I can write everything down. Since I wasn't imprinted with the ritual words I've heard about, I'll need to memorize them."

"Ready?"

"All set."

"First there is the request, where I ask you formally if you will give yourself to me to make me complete. I will ask you:

'Will you give yourself, body and soul, to complete this woman and her wolf?

'Will you unite your life with mine, bond your future with mine, and merge your half of our soul to mine, and in doing so complete the mating ritual?'

"The second part is your response,

'I will give myself, body and soul, to complete you as a woman and a wolf.

'I will unite my life with yours, bond my future to yours, and merge my half of our soul with yours.

'I will complete the mating ritual with you.'

"Then we make love as I make my vow to you:

'I claim you as my mate.

'I belong to you as you belong to me.

'I give you my heart and my body.

'I will protect you even with my life.

'I give you all I am.

'I share my half of our soul to complete you.

'I share my magic with you.' Here is where I bite your neck, then say,

'I beseech the great Luna Goddess to bless you and your wolf guardian.

'You are my mate to cherish today and for all time.

'I claim you as my mate.'

"Then you say those same words to me and bite me in the same manner. Do you have any questions?"

Thomas shook his head as he furiously wrote the last few words.

Looking closely at Thomas's hair, she slowly ran her fingers through it and watched the multitude of colors and highlights flash in the table lamp's glow. "I'm guessing you will be more of a brownish or tan wolf."

Julia's wolf voiced its approval at her assessment.

"I can hear you rumbling, babe." Thomas chuckled.

"Around you, I can't seem to help myself." She shrugged.

THOMAS: Le Beau Series

"I'm guessing since I'm in my mid–twenties; I won't have any physical changes like Mom and Rose had. I will just get my wolf soul, my wolf, and special gift. Right?"

"Yes. By the way, do you have any special abilities now as a human?"

Thomas told Julia all about his super sensor for violence and trouble. They both agreed that his sense would more than likely be enhanced by the conversion. It was a little scary to think of it getting stronger than it already was.

"Don't forget, you'll also have a longer life. Shifters live to be around fourteen hundred years old. I'm one hundred ninety myself."

"That makes you a cougar, doesn't it?" Thomas teased.

Julia gaped at him and swatted him a good one for that remark. Her flabbergasted expression made him laugh even harder.

"Hey, I just thought of something," Thomas said with a frown. "If you're one hundred sixty-five years older than me, are you going to start aging again at nine hundred and leave me behind? I don't think I like that idea."

"From what I've heard, the mates somehow sync their aging process. I will ask around to see if you will age sooner or if my aging will take longer while I wait for you to catch up."

"I don't care which way it goes as long as we do it together," Thomas said with a happy smile.

"That's my man," Julia said as she snuggled closer to him again.

"Since you're over one hundred, did you ever have to change your identity to cover up your age?"

"Only once so far. I was born with the name Emily."

"That's a pretty name. But I like Julia better."

"Thanks," Julia blushed at his compliment. "I liked being able to choose my own name verses being stuck with the one my mother chose."

Thomas was in heaven holding Julia close and watching an action movie. He couldn't imagine a better first date.

Chapter 8

The last couple days had passed quickly, and today Jack and Michael were scheduled to arrive at the Le Beau plantation after sundown. Thomas knew once the guys came to the plantation, he would be very busy, so he made a plan.

He couldn't wait another minute to see Julia again. The past two days had been agonizing, and the foreseeable future looked even less promising.

Women like surprises, right?

He thought his plan to show up unannounced was perfect. He would surprise her for a lunch date and maybe get a kiss or two.

What he hadn't expected was a hot tub...and certainly not the bikini.

Pulling his boat up to the pier at The Backwater, Thomas was hot and sweaty. March in the mountains of Colorado was cold, and snow followed by more cold and snow. In the bayou of Louisiana, the average temperature was in the seventies, and the humidity was ninety percent.

V.A. Dold

Good Lord, with this much moisture in the air, shouldn't it just rain?

As he approached her front door, he heard music on the other side of the house. He rounded the corner and daaammn! She was in a hot tub he hadn't remembered seeing the other night.

Sheeee-it! What was that song about an itsy bitsy, teeny weeny, polka dot bikini? Whatever it was, he was living it. In Technicolor, no less.

S*on–of–a–bitch*, now his tongue was numb. Had it fallen out? He glanced around his feet as if he would find it lying there.

The weather wasn't the only thing making Thomas hot.

And sweaty, and more than a little bit bothered.

Julia was relaxing with her head leaning back over the padded edge of the hot tub, eyes shut. He wasn't sure if she was napping or awake.

Apparently that distinction didn't matter to his mouth; it was watering like an out of control sprinkler over her display of enticing cleavage and curves.

It didn't seem to matter to his lower extremities either; his body had exploded to life. All he had to do was stand there and gawk for his libido to rev into overdrive.

That's when his heart started pounding, and he panicked. Should he acknowledge he was here? Or back off and pretend he'd just arrived?

Crud. What was the best way to handle this? He didn't want to be a peeping tom pervert, and yet he didn't want to lie to her either.

THOMAS: Le Beau Series

Holy cow. I am one lucky bastard, was all he could formulate in his mind as his eyes traveled over every bit of flesh he could see.

She was incredible.

He recalled the old pinup posters his father had on the walls in the garage. If he was right, they were the sex symbols of the forties. Julia would give any one of them a run for their money.

Suddenly the hair on the back of her neck stood up, and a prickle of awareness slammed through her body. Thomas was near. She slowly turned around to see if he was really there.

Aw, shit! He must have made a sound.

Julia squeaked in alarm when she saw the silhouette of a man standing at the edge of the house. With the sun at his back, she couldn't see who it was. On reflex, the items on the table beside the hot tub rose in the air, ready to do battle.

"It's me, Thomas," he quickly shouted. "Please, don't whack me with those."

"Oh." The items settled back to the tabletop as if they had never moved. Exhaling her alarm away, she watched him place his hands on his hips, as his shoulders rose and fell with the deep breaths he took. She must have startled him as badly as he had her.

He only half heard her response, thanks to the blood pounding in his ears. With her turned the way she was, he could see all of her. And he meant ALL of her from the waist up.

Holy fright!

She was in a microscopic red bikini that barely covered her nipples. A blessedly, barely there scrap of material only he would be seeing on her from this second forward. An itsy, bitsy, swimsuit he would be fantasizing about pulling off with his teeth for weeks to come. Hell, maybe months.

Damn. This was the best moment of his life. And he would be sporting wood every time he pictured her in that hot tub just like this.

Finding his brain cells, he was finally able to string words together. "Good Lord, babe," Thomas growled as he walked to the edge of the tub. "You look amazing. Those classic pin up girls from the forties have nothing on you."

Julia made an unladylike sound. "Yeah, right," she scoffed.

Thomas frowned. "I mean it. You're smoking hot." Then he quickly looked around as if to verify they were alone. "You don't let other guys see you in that bathing suit, do you?"

"Hell no! If I had known you were coming over, you wouldn't be seeing it either."

He chuckled at her disgruntled expression. "Then I'm damn glad I didn't call ahead. There's no way I would miss this view."

Thomas cupped her face and gave her a proper hello kiss.

"If my embarrassment comes with a dozen of those, I will gladly suffer the humiliation."

"You have dibs on all my kisses from now on."

"The last time a man saw me in a bikini, well, let's just say, he had some very derogatory comments. But if you like it, I'm happy to oblige."

"Who's the ass? I'll beat the crap out of him."

THOMAS: Le Beau Series

"One of the men my mother tried to pair me up with," she replied. "I'm pretty sure you're the only man who thinks these extra pounds are sexy."

He stiffened, his gut clenched at her attitude of little to no self–esteem.

"You couldn't be more wrong," he growled.

"The past six guys I was presented to by her said, and I quote, 'You're kidding, right? Where is your actual daughter? There's no way this fat chick is your pup.'"

Shock and anger coursed through Thomas. His fist clenched and unclenched, itching to strangle his not yet mother–in–law. Lucinda was a mean hearted, selfish bitch who didn't deserve her daughter. Hell, she didn't deserve oxygen.

"Your mother has a lot to answer for. I can't honestly say I'll be polite the next time I see her. There are a few things I need to straighten her out about."

"Don't waste your breath. She's too stupid or too bullheaded to hear a word that contradicts her beliefs."

"At least tell me you don't believe those bastards. You're so smoking hot I'm about to split my jeans."

"Really?" Julia said, her eyes growing hot. "Maybe I should investigate that claim?"

He nodded with a sexy grin. And it was time he made his attraction to her perfectly clear. Without the slightest hesitation, he pulled his shirt over his head and dropped his jeans.

Julia gasped as he joined her, naked as the day he was born, in the tub.

Thomas was determined to remove all doubt from her mind about just how sexy he found her. If his words wouldn't convince her, his ridged erection should go a long way to prove his point. Well, that and he planned to show her several times today through actions and words just how much a real man loved a woman with soft curves.

"You seem to be rather happy to see me," Julia giggled as he snuggled her close.

"Damn straight. And don't you forget it."

Julia had never been a forward woman, but, dang it, her smoking hot, totally ripped mate, made her sweat under the water of the hot tub. Was that even physically possible? His thumb rubbing languidly up and down her arm had her body quivering in anticipation of more intimate contact. Ah, heck. Now her mouth was getting in on the action, watering like a spigot on high over his muscled chest and abs.

"This I could get used to," Thomas said as he pulled her onto his very naked lap. No imagination needed there.

Thomas's gaze was smoldering and burned with his unspoken lust.

Holy smokes! He really is turned on by my body.

Yes. I am. And don't you ever forget it, woman.

"This sure is pretty, what are you drinking?" Thomas asked, examining her pink and blue cocktail.

She passed her glass to him so he could taste it as she answered. "A Kinky Hook Up."

Mid–swallow and he was choking and sputtering like a blue haired old lady at the porno movie.

"A what?" he asked as he caught his breath.

Julia laughed as his reaction. "A Kinky Hook Up. It's Kinky pink, Kinky blue, with lemon–lime soda. They're really yummy. Most of the guys at the bar would never admit it, but they order them all the time."

"It is tasty, not that I would admit that in public, mind you," he grinned and then teased her. "Men require macho drinks, like whiskey in a shot glass."

"Oh, they do?"

"Heck, yeah. We have reputations to uphold. Otherwise someone might try to kick our ass. Oh, yeah. That already happened."

Julia blushed and wiggled off his lap. "Sorry about that."

Before he could stop her, she was out of the hot tub and wrapped in a towel.

"I'm going to get some clothes on." Silently she walked to the house.

When she came down the hall from her bedroom, Thomas was waiting in the living room. Fully dressed, thank Goddess.

"What just happened here?" he asked with confusion etched across his features.

"I'm pretty sure the attack on you was my fault. Or, should I say, my mother's."

"If that was orchestrated by Lucinda, it wasn't your fault."

"Maybe so, but she did it to keep me from dating a human. So, essentially it was kind of my fault."

"Babe, look at me." He lifted her chin with one gentle finger. "Her actions are not your fault or responsibility. She will have to answer for that if she is found responsible. Do you understand me?"

Julia nodded.

"Good." Taking her by the hand, he led her to the loveseat. "If you have a few minutes, I wanted to talk to you about a few things."

"All right." His sexy, deep voice sent goosebumps over her arms, not to mention raised her blood pressure to a dangerous level. "What about?"

"Well, for one thing, that incredible sexy bikini is officially for my eyes only," he stated, a smile evident in his tone. "As manly and strong as I am, I can't spend my time beating men off you twenty–four seven."

His dimples dazzled her as he smiled wide. Dimples she hadn't seen before, mainly because he'd never really smiled like this before. That smile was something she planned on seeing a lot. It made her heart stutter and stomach flutter.

"You sure are beautiful when you look at me like that."

Julia just grinned at him and snuggled into his side. *Goddess, I love those dimples, but no need to give him a big head over it.*

You like my dimples, huh.

Shit.

Thomas laughed at her bright pink cheeks as he tucked a stray hair behind her ear.

"You keep looking at me like that, and I'll never get around to telling you why I came over."

Heat flashed down her neck and lower as she tried to hide her embarrassment.

As if he could see through her clothing he said, "I love it when you blush. But, I wonder if the pretty color goes all the way down to more – interesting places?"

She smacked him on the arm, and he chuckled again.

"I wanted to see you today before Jack and Michael arrive at the plantation. Etienne says they are ready to join the security team, and I need to have a meeting with them and Isaac before we can move forward."

"So why did you need to see me first?" Julia frowned.

"Based on what Etienne was telling me, his training crew is in Las Vegas. He feels we will be much more effective as a team if we train and practice together with his crew for a few weeks. That way I can learn the vampires' abilities and how best to blend them with the shifters."

Julia became very quiet. "I see."

"I hate to leave you right now, but it can't be helped. How about we plan a date night for the day I come home?"

His suggestion lightened the weight on her chest a bit. "Okay. What did you have in mind?"

"I have an early flight back three Mondays from now, so how about dinner in the Quarter? You pick the restaurant, and I'll make reservations."

"How about Irene's?"

"Great! I love Italian food. Before I leave, can I get your work schedule? I'd like to call you or Skype when you have free time. I'd hate to bother you at work."

Julia wrote out her schedule for the next three weeks with a sad heart. Being away from him that long was going to kill her. Not that she would tell him that. He had a job to do, and she wouldn't cause him any guilt doing it.

"Here you go," she said as cheerfully as she could.

"Thanks, babe." Thomas pulled her in for a long toe– curling kiss before he leaned his forehead against hers. "Damn, I hate the thought of not seeing you for so long. Will you be okay? This isn't going to cause you pain, is it?"

Julia knew she had to lie; otherwise he would refuse to go. "No, of course not. I'll be fine."

All he had to do was ask any shifter, and he would know the truth. Her mate being that far away without the ritual completed would be excruciating.

Chapter 9

The past few hours had been the best of Thomas's life and would have to tide him over for the next twenty–one days. How had he gone from dead set against a relationship to not being able to live without his woman? Heck, he hadn't even gotten her into his bed yet, and he could barely breathe without her. This mating thing was crazy, and scary, and awesome, all at the same time.

Checking his watch, he had thirty minutes before the meeting at Grandpa's. That was just enough time to grab a sandwich and a change of clothes. Daydreaming about his woman came with very wet, very smelly, consequences. A few minutes ago, as he stepped from the dock, he'd found himself shin deep in swamp stank. The images of her bikini flashing through his mind should have come with a hazard warning. He was really going to have to work on his attention skills.

Thirty minutes later, Thomas heard the crowd in Grandpa Isaac's office before he rounded the corner. It sounded like everyone except him was already present.

Good, he hated waiting for people who couldn't manage to tell time.

"Thomas!" Both Jack and Michael greeted him the second he crossed the threshold.

"It's great to see you looking so well," he greeted them back.

Fist bumps and man hugs were energetically exchanged. He had really missed these guys.

Turning to the leaders present, he said, "It looks like we just need John, and we're ready."

As always, Etienne was more regal and simply gave him a nod in recognition. And, of course, Grandpa smiled proudly from behind his desk.

A second later, John stepped through the door, prompt as usual. Of course as children, Thomas had to beat punctuality into his little brother or else their father would do worse. But now, as an adult, John was never late if he could help it.

Isaac cleared his throat, and everyone took a seat.

"I think it would be best to bring Thomas and John up to speed on Jack and Michael's gifts, as well as limitations,"

Etienne nodded his approval. "I agree. First and foremost, a young vampire cannot be in daylight. That ability comes with age and generally is available to vampires two hundred years and older. As thus, my men will be best suited for night work. They will need to feed at least once a week to maintain their strength. Otherwise, their diet is as normal as any of yours. Unlike the vampires of fantasy, we do not die in order to be converted and can survive for long stretches of time without blood at all. But to maintain our strength and speed we need to feed regularly."

THOMAS: Le Beau Series

"What kind of strength and speed are you talking about? Are you fast like a shifter?" John asked.

"We can move so swiftly, you would think we had teleported. Our strength is equal to twenty human men. That was one of the main reasons the boys had to stay away from you and your families. As a newborn, a vampire must learn how to touch things without crushing them. It sounds ludicrous, but that is the way of it."

"What other gifts do they bring to the security team?" Thomas asked with his notepad in hand.

"They can become invisible by bending the light so human eyes can not detect them. I am told a shifter's eyes can still see us but not a human's. We discovered, quite by accident, that if several vampires form a circle and become invisible at the same time, it creates a bubble. Anything within the bubble is both invisible and sound proof.

I have taught both Jack and Michael mind control and programming. Very few vampires are trained in these gifts to maintain order in the power system we have created. But these two are like sons to me and as such, have my complete trust."

Thomas finished scribbling his notes and glanced at Etienne again. "Are there any other gifts I should know about?"

"The three of us have exchanged blood in order to read each others' minds and speak telepathically. If you would like them to be able to read your mind for security purposes, you will need to let each of them take a small amount of blood. Sadly, you will not be able to do the same since taking their blood would initiate your conversion to vampire. The best you would achieve is one way communication."

V.A. Dold

"So, it's your blood, not the actual bite that converts? I was wondering about that," John said.

"Yes, no one has pinpointed what exactly is in a vampires blood to cause the conversion. Even we have tried to understand the cause and effect but it remains a mystery."

"What do you tell your new vampires and other supernaturals?" John asked as he sat forward, fascinated by the topic.

"We remain relegated to calling it magic," Etienne quipped with a twinkle in his eye.

Isaac barked out a laugh at his old friend's dry sense of humor.

"One last caution, a vampire is still a complete man if you get my point. Don't be surprised by my men in Las Vegas having girlfriends and wives or boyfriends as the situation dictates. A few even have children. I own a block on the strip where I built a luxury condo high–rise for my family's housing. I have assigned each of you a unit for the duration of your stay. There is a training facility below ground in the lower levels that has everything you will need and is available for your use at any time. The building is equipped with windows made of a customized two–way mirror substance. It blocks the harmful rays from the sun and looks like mirrored glass to the human eye. This protects the young vampires while allowing them to see daylight, which they would never have enjoyed a decade ago. It is not a perfect solution but better than we had before."

Thomas was nodding along and taking notes as fast as he could. "What are our travel plans to get there and back while avoiding daylight?"

Isaac stood and rounded his desk. "I've already filed a flight plan for the Le Beau private jet. The plane will keep Jack and Michael safe while providing the discretion we require."

"What about housing when we return? Do you have a plan in motion?" Thomas asked the consummate organizer.

"Jack and Michael have provided blueprints for their houses and we'll begin building while you are away. If we finish the lower levels first, they can live in them while we complete the above ground portion. Living in a construction zone isn't the most pleasant but we'll complete construction as quickly as possible."

"If I may, I would like to offer a night crew so the construction may continue around the clock. That way the houses will be completed close to their return or fairly soon after."

"That's a great idea. Have your foreman meet with mine to plan the shifts."

Thomas rubbed his hands together. "I guess that only leaves one thing, what time do we take off? I still need to pack."

Jack finally joined the conversation then. "Two hours, just after dusk."

"We would help but..." Michael joked.

"Yeah. Yeah." John laughed. "You just hang out and drink Grandpa's scotch. We'll be back in about an hour."

Few people knew of the private airfield and family jet kept there. Now, two more were added to that very short list of people in the know. Jack and Michael boarded with John and Thomas as Isaac and Etienne watched over the airfield. When security was a prime concern, secrecy was imperative.

The flight from the plantation to Las Vegas was blessedly short. Etienne's man in charge of his Las Vegas family waited patiently beside an already prepped helicopter.

Thomas grinned as he thought *these vampires are the most organized group I've ever met.*

The neon lights of the strip where almost blinding from above. Thomas glanced at John and the vampires; the brightness must be too much for their sensitive eyes. Each wore pitch–black sunglasses, so dark, he wondered if they could see at all.

The family compound was built almost dead center of the current city sprawl. Between the placement and height of the structure, the high–rise afforded the vampires a leg up in maintaining control of the entire area. Thomas's admiration increased ten fold; Etienne was a damn smart man and warrior.

The rooftop was astounding: gardens, pools with waterfalls, the ultimate oasis from the frenetic energy that coursed through the veins of the city of sin. With a refuge like this, he just might enjoy his three weeks here.

Within seconds of disembarking the helicopter, it lifted off and disappeared into the night. Three additional vampires joined them and escorted each of their party to their private suite.

Daaamn!

His suite could have given any high roller's penthouse in the city a run for its money. Etienne sure believed in giving his family every comfort and convenience. The only thing it was missing was Julia.

THOMAS: Le Beau Series

Finished unpacking, he knocked on John's door. Thank goodness he was next door, this place was massive, and he didn't care to prowl the halls looking for his crew. John's suite was decorated in earth tones where as his was blues and greens, otherwise they were very similar.

"Hey, bro. This is awesome!" John exclaimed.

"Mine, too."

Moments later, Jack and Michael knocked on the door.

"They would like to give us a tour if you are done unpacking," Michael said, as he sauntered through the open door.

John cocked his head as he studied the men closely for the first time. "Y'all move differently than you used too."

"Yeah, you do," Thomas agreed.

"All part of the vampire charm," Jack grinned. "We move with a gliding kind of walk rather than a human walk."

Michael nodded. "We figured that influenced the fictional portrayal of vampires floating. Although the crazy powerful vampires like Etienne really can float. It's actually kind of creepy to witness."

"Enough vampire folklore." Jack laughed. "Let's get this tour started. How about the boring facts first? The building is fifty stories above ground and eight below. The top story is Etienne's personal penthouse, and directly below that is reserved for his personal guests. All other floors are either individual family units, meeting rooms or training space. All except basement eight that is reserved for – well let's call them –

V.A. Dold

'encouragement rooms'. You never want to find yourself a guest in one of those rooms."

Michael laughed along with Jack. "That's for sure."

"You saw the helipad when we landed. What you didn't see was the rooftop pool and putting green."

Thomas looked from Jack to Michael and laughed. "A putting green?"

Michael shook his head. "You'd never guess it, but Etienne is addicted to golf."

Once the laughter and jokes quieted down, Jack continued. "You'll see the practice rooms and gyms when we head down for our first workout. In the meantime, would you like to see the different styles of condos or how about we kick back with a cocktail in the lounge on the seventh floor?"

"Cocktail," both John and Thomas said at the same time.

After a relaxing beer, the sun was still too high in the sky, and the young vampires were forced to remain indoors. Thomas decided they should have a short training meeting. A plan of action and schedule would go a long way in getting the men back to Louisiana as soon as possible.

Armed with a list of Jack's and Michael's abilities and weaknesses, Thomas returned to his suite to formulate teams and strategies so he could plan maneuvers he wanted them to practice.

An hour later, John found him deep in paperwork and hand-drawn diagrams that look more like football plays than security procedures.

"You ready to take a break and check out the strip?"

"Give me a minute, I'm almost done."

THOMAS: Le Beau Series

Give Thomas an inch, and he'll take a mile when it came to planning and security measures. Five minutes later, John snatched the pen from a very disgruntled Thomas and demanded he take a break.

He was finally able to convince John to return to the compound when the sunset colored the sky.

"All right, bro. I've had enough sightseeing of barely clad women. You may still be single, but I'm a taken man. We need to head back."

"You're serious about Julia? I heard a rumor she was your mate, but I never can tell if Stefan is pulling my leg or not."

"Yep. She is, but so far we're taking it slow. I never planned to have a girlfriend much less a wife or mate. Don't get me wrong, I'm not having second thoughts, just taking my time and getting to know her. Fourteen hundred years is a long time with a woman. And if you met her mother, you'd take your time, too."

"That bad?"

"Worse."

Back in his suite, after a shower and change into clean boxers, Thomas tried calling Julia. She must still be at The Backwater. He really hated voicemail and left a quick message before ending the call.

A few minutes later his phone rang. "Hello?"

"Hello, cher. I'm sorry I missed your call. How was the flight to Las Vegas?"

Her drowsy voice sounded like heaven to his ears. Or, at least he imagined that must be what heaven would sound like. Visions of his woman stretched before him, wearing nothing but satin sheets materialized in his mind. He'd never touched satin sheets, but he had seen them in movies often enough to have a pretty good idea how much he'd like to get her naked in them with nothing between him and all her delectable skin. Her hair fanned out over the pillow and lips swollen with his kisses. Candlelight playing lovingly over her curves and lighting the love that burned in her eyes.

"God, I miss you already," he breathed, his voice gravelly with need. He was going to have a long sleepless night if he didn't take care of the raging hard-on he was sporting just hearing her voice.

"I miss you, too."

He heard what sounded like a small gasp and a hint of pain in her voice.

"You okay? Are you hurt?"

"No," she answered a little too quickly. "I'm just tired." She tried to cover up her pain from the separation of her mate and her stupid panicked response. She didn't want him returning early because of her. This trip was too important to him and the security of her uncle.

"Maybe you need to hire another bartender and work fewer hours?"

"I have been considering it. I was going to talk to Logan about it tomorrow."

"Good, I don't want you overworking yourself. Besides, when I get back, I plan to take you out on plenty of dates, so you're gonna need a lot of nights off."

"Is that right?" she teased.

"Damn straight. Now get some sleep and dream of me. I'll talk to you tomorrow."

"You get some sleep too, and stay away from the women in that town."

"No worries there, babe. You're the only one for me."

"I appreciate you saying that, Believe it or not, I don't have the highest self-esteem."

"Sweetheart, there is no one in this world more beautiful than you. Believe me when I say, I don't even see those women out there showing off their bodies like they're selling themselves. Even John was sick of it by the time I told him I wanted to go back to our rooms."

"You think I'm pretty?"

"No."

There was a long pause. "No?" she asked quietly.

"No. I think you're beautiful. Lots of girls are pretty, but few are truly beautiful."

He heard Julia sniffle. "Are you crying? I'm sorry, babe. Did I say something wrong?"

"You said everything right."

"And that made you cry?"

"These are happy tears. Why don't men get that?"

"You're going to have to clue me in on all this girl stuff."

"You got it, cher. As soon as you get home we can start your lessons."

"Aw, now that just ain't right, talking dirty to me over the phone when I can't do anything about it," he teased.

"Maybe tomorrow instead of phone sex we could have Skype sex?"

Thomas about swallowed his tongue.

"Tommy? You still there?"

All he could do was grunt in response.

Julia laughed at his antics. "How about I call you tomorrow after work, maybe you will be able to speak by then."

He cleared his sex–fogged brain. "Yeah, okay, that sounds great."

"Good night, cher."

"Good night, babe."

He hung up the phone grinning like a fool, good luck sleeping tonight with that visual of Skype sex still floating around in his head.

*****

Two hours of tossing and turning and still images of Julia danced like sugar plums in his head. Suddenly he stilled and listened hard. Was that John? He thought John had gotten past the nightmares.

Throwing back the covers he paced to their shared wall and leaned closer. Something that felt like a knife twisted hard and painfully in Thomas's chest as he heard John's anguish again.

John had given him a key to his room earlier so Thomas could let himself in. It was easier than getting up to answer the door twelve times a day as Thomas came and went.

As Thomas quietly came through the door, John raised his head from his knees. He had them pulled tightly to his chest as he sat up against the headboard of his bed and rocked himself. The relived horror in his dream still too raw, was stark in his eyes.

Thomas knew what it was like to huddle in his room; voices raised in anger between his parents. He vividly recalled watching his father systematically break his mother's heart and tear down her self–esteem. Not only his mother, his entire family, broken by his abusive father.

THOMAS: Le Beau Series

As a child, he hid the shame of his father's behavior from classmates and friends. Eventually, as the abuse escalated from mental abuse to physical, he isolated both himself and John from his father by building a secret hideout in the hills behind their home. The moment his father showed up, which wasn't often the last few years, he hustled John out the backdoor, and they didn't return until the bastard left.

Running and hiding made him feel like a coward. It really grated on his conscience that his mother was left alone to take his father's abuse alone. It wasn't until years later that his mother eased his guilt when she told them their absence had allowed her to fight back against his father. Apparently, he was such a coward; he could only beat on children. Adults were off the menu, so thankfully he never hit his mother. He hadn't known it at the time, but she held back while her sons were present, sparing them the memory of their mother ripping into their father and shredding him to bits. Anna was a force to be reckoned with when cornered.

"The bastard can't hurt you anymore."

"I know. Maybe you could tell that to the nightmares."

Thomas nodded his head. "It's because we're in Vegas and he's here somewhere isn't it?"

"I suppose so."

Chapter 10

Last night had been a rough one, neither he nor John had gotten much sleep, staying up and talking through their issues with their father the entire night. He hoped John would sleep better tonight. It was only eight a.m. and already lights out couldn't come soon enough.

The team had breakfast at nine and then training until noon with a two hour break before another round of training into the evening. That was the schedule they would live by for the duration. Thomas made an executive decision during the night, as soon as training was done, regardless of how many days it took, they were going home. As much as he appreciated Etienne and his crew, Las Vegas didn't agree with him or John.

*****

Julia knew she was in trouble, Tommy had only been gone for twenty–four hours, and already she was daydreaming about him every second she got. There was no getting him out of her head. He hovered there, like a moth to a flame, a living, breathing, wet dream, in her thoughts.

THOMAS: Le Beau Series

Every fiber of her being wanted to jump on a plane and hunt him down. The constant pain from the distance between her and her mate wasn't helping either and blocking that from Thomas was exhausting.

"What the heck is wrong with you today?" Logan huffed from behind the bar.

"What?" Julia asked as she shook off the fog named Tommy.

"You're washing that same table for the third time. What gives?"

"Can't concentrate I guess."

In one smooth leap, Logan cleared the bar with ease. Lifting her chin, he searched her eyes. "How bad is it?"

"I'll survive."

"That's not what I asked."

"I can manage the pain, it's missing him I'm struggling with."

Logan gave her one last hard look and released her chin and walked back to the bar. "If you don't snap out of it, I'm going to call him."

Julia whirled around, "Don't. You. Dare."

"You may be hell on wheels, and a pain in my ass, little sister, but I won't have you suffering."

He held her gaze until she looked away. She was going to have to suck it up, or Logan would do just what he threatened. Taking a deep breath, she cleared the cobwebs from her brain and made sure she didn't do anything stupid the rest of her shift.

In a few hours, she would see Tommy by Skype. She prayed that interacting, even if only electronically, would ease the pain and help her concentrate.

V.A. Dold

*****

Seven fifty-five p.m., five more minutes, and she would be talking to Tommy! Time slowed to a crawl until Julia was ready to scream. Every tick from her clock boomed like thunder in her ears as the longest five minutes of her life dragged on.

Just when she thought she would go insane, her laptop dinged, announcing a Skype call.

"Tommy?" Julia called out, as she clicked the answer button.

"Oh, baby. You are a sight for sore eyes." Thomas sighed, then he frowned. "Are you feeling okay? You look a little pale and tired."

"I miss you like crazy. I am a little tired, but that's all. I'm okay, really." Julia was quick to assure him. She didn't want him to cut his trip short because she was a little uncomfortable. Okay, a lot uncomfortable, but she wasn't going to admit that to anyone.

The way he searched her face she was afraid he would see through her fib. Finally, his sexy lips stretched into a smile.

Whew, she exhaled the breath she had been holding.

"You're all I think about. Being away from you, it hurts in a way I wouldn't have imagined. Hans almost impaled me in practice today because I was fantasizing about you instead of paying attention. I need to hold you in my arms," he admitted quietly.

"I need you too, but it's only for a couple weeks. And you really need to pay attention in class, I don't want you full of holes when you get back."

Seconds later, a wicked thought flitted in the back of her mind. "Take off your shirt."

Thomas's eyes shot to hers, "What?"

THOMAS: Le Beau Series

"Take it off, big boy."

A steamy gleam heated his eyes as he slowly unbuttoned his shirt. His breathing increased, watching her lick her lips with her eyes fastened on the ever–increasing gap he was creating.

He could see her skin beginning to flush. When the buttons were all undone, he looked her in the eye and quietly said, "Tell me what you want."

"Take it all the way off," she breathed

Thomas let the shirt slide off his arms and back, to find its way to the floor. He watched her gaze devour him. Damn, he was never going to live through this. He waited for her to look at him again.

After what felt like forever, her eyes returned to his. "What do you have on under that pretty blouse, babe?"

Julia chewed her lower lip blushing for so many long seconds he thought she was going to chicken out. Just when he thought he was going to go to bed hard as a rock and horny as hell, she started unbuttoning.

His breath hitched when the edges gaped enough to show a lacy pink bra. Her nipples strained against the material, two dark, tempting buds, waiting for his attention.

Her eyes returned to his as she boldly let the blouse float to the floor. Running her fingers along the upper edge of the left cup she held his gaze and slowly reached behind with her right hand to pop the clasp.

Lord have mercy.

The bra burst loose, the release causing her breasts to bob enticingly, and she let the scrap fall.

He licked his lips. "You're incredible, Julia. Damn woman, you're killing me, I want to taste you so badly." Thomas adjusted his position in his chair to alleviate the pressure building behind the zipper.

Julia quirked a little-wicked smile as she rolled her nipples and caressed the round, plump globes he wanted to touch in person.

His breathing increased with each touch.

"Take your jeans off, cher. Let me see you."

Thomas rose from the desk chair, the bulge behind his zipper blatantly evident. All Julia could see was from his waistband to mid thigh. His hands entered the viewing area, and she watched his fingers work the button and lower the zipper. At the rate her breathing was accelerating, she just might hyperventilate.

She ached to see his face, but at the same time, her gaze was locked on his lower region. She almost stopped breathing altogether when his thumbs hooked inside the waistband, and he slid the blue jeans out of view.

A distant, detached voice growled. "Tell me what you want, Julia."

How could her mouth be watering and dry as the desert at the same time?

"Remove your boxers. I want to see all of you," she managed to croak.

Those thumbs appeared on screen again, hitching into the waistband and lowering the offending boxers a fraction of an inch at a time.

When Julia growled her impatience, Thomas laughed a low sexy chuckle and finished stripping the boxers away. As the elastic cleared his engorged erection, it snagged on the head, when it popped loose the action caused his aching cock to bounce.

Julia actually whimpered in frustration.

THOMAS: Le Beau Series

Thomas leaned down to look into the camera. "I'm going to get a washcloth, this could get messy. I'll be right back."

Moments later he returned and took his seat before the monitor. Holding her gaze, he quietly demanded. "Now it's your turn. I want to see all of you."

Julia searched his eyes for a minute chewing on her fingernail. All the while he slowly stroked his aching erection.

Can I do this? She wasn't a wilting flower; she was Lady Julia Le Beau. *Of course, she could do this.*

Following Tommy's lead, she stripped off her jeans and panties. For added measure, she tossed her matching pink lacy thong at the webcam.

Tommy's eyes looked like they were going to pop out of his face they were so large. And his mouth hung open as he stared at her now naked body. She wanted to cover up so badly, but she held her head high and let him look his fill.

"My God! I am one lucky bastard. You are exquisite."

She laughed when he wiped the edges of his mouth to make sure he wasn't drooling.

"Touch yourself, babe. I want to watch you please yourself."

Thomas couldn't take his eyes off her as she rolled and tweaked her nipples before sliding one hand between her legs. He watched her face intently as she slid her fingers into her channel and stroked out again to rub her swollen clit. Over and over, the tension and pleasure built. Their eyes glazed over, and heads fell back as each of their climaxes began to roar through their bodies. Thomas held the washcloth over his cock to catch his release; it wouldn't do to leave such a personal mess in one of Etienne's condos.

Julia cried out his name as she came. Her shout and shuddering body took him over the edge with her.

"Julia!"

Thomas's release exploded into the waiting cloth, capturing the evidence of their very naughty Skype encounter.

Neither could breathe for a minute, both panting, eyes closed, with satisfied smiles on their faces.

"I can't wait to be the one making you scream like that," Thomas panted.

"I can't wait to touch you, and make love to you, either," Julia agreed.

*****

Thomas ran his fingers through his hair, grinning as he sipped his first cup of coffee. Morning fifteen brought a new level of excitement. He was running timed maneuvers today, and if the team did well enough they would be headed home tomorrow. The next twenty–four hours couldn't pass fast enough.

His pulse raced and jeans tightened, imagining Julia's welcome home kiss. He couldn't wait to surprise her. Their first real date was long over due, and he had a night to remember in the French Quarter planned for them.

Thomas walked into the training room an hour later and laid out the day's schedule. The teams excitement level ratcheted up a notch with each completed maneuver. Every one executed to perfection. By lunch they were done and flight plans home were being arranged.

THOMAS: Le Beau Series

"You want to hit the strip one last time with me?" John asked.

His expression and tone were so hopeful Thomas couldn't say no. "Sure, why not. I'll meet you in the lobby in thirty."

Thomas did his best to look like he was enjoying the barhopping fest that John was dragging him along on. A couple of weeks ago, he would have been all in, but now that he had Julia, the bars didn't hold the same appeal.

It took a moment to adjust his eyes to the bright afternoon sun as they exited their fourth club. When they walked in, a stripper who eerily resembled Julia took the stage. Thomas had been so uncomfortable they only stayed for one beer and were now on the sidewalk again.

"Let's hit Bellagio before we head back," John said.

"Cool." Thomas nodded. "I'd like to see that fountain show, like in 'Ocean's Eleven'."

They were recounting scenes from the movie when Thomas felt a tingle run up his neck. Slowly he turned; Tim, their father, wasn't more than twenty feet away, manhandling a woman young enough to be their sister.

The color drained from John's face as he stood frozen, the terror of his childhood memories etched on his face.

Thomas gently touched John's shoulder and moved him into the shadows of an awning. "Stay here, I'll handle this."

In truth, he hadn't seen or heard from Tim since Etienne banished him to Las Vegas. Except for John's nightmares, he hadn't given the bastard a moment's thought. It hadn't occurred to him his father would victimize another woman or child; he had simply been ecstatic to be rid of him. He wanted to kick himself, he should have known it was more than likely, and he'd make sure it didn't happen again.

Tim was a mean, little son of a bitch, who liked to beat on those weaker than himself in order to feel like a big man. Well, not anymore. Thomas squared his shoulders. This ended here.

"Let her go," he growled coldly.

Tim turned his body language shouting this was none of your business until he recognized the face of his enemy. "Well, look who we have here. Where's your punk brother, John?" he asked, searching the sidewalk for his missing son.

Tim's eyes were emotionless, cold, pits, staring at him. He was used to intimidating his rivals, smaller rivals that is. Too bad it didn't work on him. Hadn't for a very long time.

Out of the corner of his eye, he saw the terrified woman shudder. Her fear flipped a switch he hadn't known he had. Tim enjoyed inflicting pain. Well now, he was about to be on the receiving end.

"I said, let her go. I won't say it again."

Tim let out a snort. "What do you think you're going to do about it? If I remember correctly, you ran scared when ever I came around."

"Take a good long look, 'Dad'." Thomas sneered. "Do you really think I'm going to run now?"

Tim's eyes bulged as if he were seeing his oldest son as a grown man for the first time. Thomas actually watched the horror register in his father's eyes when he realized he was totally screwed.

John chose that moment to face his fears and stand shoulder to shoulder with Thomas.

THOMAS: Le Beau Series

Two things happened simultaneously. The woman was shoved into John's chest, and Thomas slammed his fist into Tim's nose. Tim's head flew back as blood splattered both men. As if in slow motion, the bastard crumbled like a house of cards in a light breeze.

With a fist full of his father's shirt, Thomas snarled, "Get her out of here."

John gave him a single nod; all the childhood fear gone from his eyes and led the woman into the nearest doorway.

Several vampires materialized from the shadows, creating a visual blockade around the two men. Perfect, he could take care of this scum without witnesses.

Thomas turned his piercing blue gaze directly on his sperm donor. Leaning in, Tim's rancid breath was hot on his face.

"It's time you got a little payback from one of your victims," he stated, his voice harsh.

There was a ridged set to his chin and a scowl creased his brow. He was merciless with a deadly, ruthless resolve clearly carved on his face.

Without sparing a glance to Hans, the leader of this team of vampires, he growled. "Keep us out of sight and don't let anyone hear this."

"It will be our pleasure, but perhaps we should move this to a less public location. I suggest the alley behind you," Hans responded with humor in his tone. "My only regret is, our king forbids his death, at least by our hand."

The vampires hated Tim as much as Thomas and John did.

Thomas pulled Tim to his feet and shoved him toward the opening the vampires had created in their circle. Tim's only choice was the alley, and he was more than willing to take it.

Without a second thought, he turned and ran. No doubt hoping for an exit to appear within the rank narrow space. He was wrong.

Where before Thomas had been a victim of this scum, now the victimizer was his prey. He allowed his father a moment of fruitless hope, prolonging the fear he knew the man was feeling.

Paybacks were a bitch, and he purposely took his time tracking Tim down to add to his fear and torment. Sometimes the uncertainty of what was to come was as much torture as the final pain you received. And Tim deserved everything he was about to get.

Long moments passed. The sound of traffic and a car horn blast were all that broke the silence. He patiently waited until the aggressive energy coming from the alley dissipated. He wanted Tim to think he had a chance, wanted him to have false hope, so he could snatch it from him like he had done to him and John so many times. And, there it was.

Tommy?

Thomas heard the terror in Julia's voice, but he couldn't deal with it right now. With an ability he hadn't realized he had, he slammed a wall in place. Effectively blocking Julia from his mind and what was about to happen.

Menace radiated from him as he cracked his neck and walked to the mouth of the alley. A quick appraisal of the cardboard box and trash littered space told him there was only one hiding spot afforded to the bastard. A filthy dumpster jammed against the left wall.

THOMAS: Le Beau Series

The trash and broken glass crunched under Thomas's boots as he took his time walking to the far side of the trash bin where he knew he would find Tim. An occasional rat scurried from under the trash as it sensed the predators filling the small space and ran for safer cover.

He stopped short of rounding the dumpster. "Are you going to be a man and come out on your own two feet, or do I need to drag your pathetic ass out?"

"Fuck you," Tim shouted in a quavering voice.

Thomas sighed and took the final steps needed to see the pathetic excuse that was his father crouched between the wall and the dumpster. Tim's shirt was drenched with sweat, no doubt from fear and the smell of urine was strong, the asshat had wet himself.

Thomas took hold of a leg and dragged a screeching Tim into the center of the alley. Slowly the vampires closed the circle, giving Thomas the visual and audio barrier he needed.

Tim's eyes flashed around the small circle as if an exit would magically appear. Grabbing the front of Tim's shirt, Thomas hauled him to his feet. "Look at me, you piece of shit. I want to see the fear in your eyes."

Tim reluctantly tore his eyes from the vampires to glare at Thomas. That glare instantly turned to terror as recognition of his impending death filled his eyes.

"Please, son. Don't hurt me. I'm your father, for Christ sake."

"You should have felt that sentiment when I was a child, and as a father not beat your children. The road runs both ways, Daddy," Thomas sneered.

In one fluid motion, Thomas stepped to Tim and hammered him with a flurry of blows to the face and body. His father must have been loaded with meth or some other street drug; the fear in the man's eyes shifted toward insanity. He acted as if he hadn't felt the blows, and even managed to nail Thomas with a hard uppercut to the jaw. The two went at it like roosters in a cockfight. Like All–Star wrestlers, they used the circle of vampires as ropes in a boxing ring, bouncing off and slamming the other mercilessly.

Their faces were harsh masks of hatred, lips peeled back, and rage filled eyes. Death lived in their expressions.

A vicious blow from Thomas had Tim stumbling against a huge Asian vampire. With an angry snap of his fangs, the vampire shoved Tim toward the center of the circle.

His father's clumsy movements masked the fact he was armed. The setting sun glinted off the old steel for only a fraction of a second when he pulled the battered blade from a back pocket of his grubby jeans.

A combination of stumbling and lurching brought Tim in contact with Hans. His flailing actions were so ridiculous; Hans hadn't afforded the enemy proper attention and now sported a sliced arm as his reward. A wicked, ragged, blistering cut that looked like it burned and must have stung like hell.

The wound wouldn't kill him, but that didn't mean it didn't hurt like a son of a bitch. The fucking knife must be coated with a shabby silver plating.

Hurling himself across the ring of men, Thomas knocked Tim off of Hans. The force of the blow knocked the knife from his hand, and his momentum landed them on the filthy pavement with Thomas on Tim's chest. A quick swing of his left leg and he straddled the bastard.

THOMAS: Le Beau Series

He pulled his fists back and pummeled Tim's face with everything he had. The smacks of fist meeting flesh were followed by pained groans. His fury was so focused; he blocked out the ring of vampires surrounding them. He continued to punish the bastard until Tim's face was unrecognizable pulp and his knuckles were raw.

Hans sensed Thomas's resolve to annihilate his father. Thomas's fist was drawn, ready to deliver the killing blow. Tim was nearly finished as it was. His nose twisted in a painful angle to the right. The human bled so heavily; it just might bleed out. He could only hope.

"I'm going to kill you for everything you ever did to John and Mom," Thomas growled.

Hans grabbed his arm. "Brother, you don't want to do that."

Thomas struggled with indecision. Finally, he lowered his fist, breathing heavily. Two of Hans's men helped him to his feet and away from his worthless father.

Though Thomas both agreed and disagreed with Hans, he wanted Tim dead but at the same time, he didn't care to live with his father's death on his hands. His whole body continued to shake with adrenaline, and his eyes remained dark with rage. Gasping for breath, his chest heaved, and angry energy poured from him, filling the narrow alley with its stench.

"Thomas, as much as this filth deserves to die," Hans snarled. "I prefer you enjoy your life without the guilt you would no doubt feel if you personally killed this piece of shit. Let us leave that for another day, and gift another person with his death."

Aggression still had Thomas revved up and spitting mad. With hatred coursing through his veins, he clenched and unclenched his fists.

Why am I sticky?

When he looked down, he saw the bloody mess he'd made of his hands and clothing. He flexed his fingers a couple of times and felt the ache beginning to settle in now that he was coming down from the adrenaline high of the fight. This was going to hurt like a bitch in about an hour. A sharp pain in his left hand indicated he might have broken a finger or two, but at this moment in time he didn't care. He considered wiping the blood on Tim, but the tacky Hawaiian shirt he wore was soaked through, and there wasn't an inch of clean fabric remaining.

Hans directed his men to move Tim into the shadows, behind the dumpster. He could come to, lying in the filth of the alleyway. Not that the he deserved to draw another breath.

As Thomas turned to go, he yelled over his shoulder, "That's how it feels to get your ass handed to you, asshole. Remember that when you feel like hitting a woman or child again, you fucking piece of shit. Because if you don't, one of us will give you a refresher."

Thomas thought he might have heard a moan in response, but he wasn't sure and didn't care one way or the other.

Julia? Can you hear me?

He felt the distance like a tangible fog. Yeah. She was there; it was slight but he could sense her energy in their link.

Tommy? I'm here. Are you okay? I feel pain radiating from you.

THOMAS: Le Beau Series

He didn't answer her question; he didn't want her to worry. Instead, he closed his eyes briefly, allowing the sound of her voice to wash through his mind and sooth his damaged soul. His heart ached and his body tightened, but her voice cured all. He picked up the pace, moving quickly through the streets, taking the shortest possible route back to his suite.

Can I Skype you in about twenty minutes? I really need to see your face.

I'll be here, mon amour.

Thomas ran the few blocks back to the condo. He needed to put distance between himself and his father almost as much as he needed to see Julia.

One look in the vanity mirror, as he stepped into his bathroom, told him he would need a shower and new clothes before Julia laid eyes on him. Already, his shirt was hardening and crusty from the blood, and his hair was matted with gore and bits of trash.

A quiet knock sounded followed by a click as John unlocked the condo door and gaped at him.

"I'm surprised the cops didn't pick me up looking like this."

"Do you need a doctor?" John asked gently, and then he snarled. "Tell me the bastard is dead."

Thomas clasped John's shoulder as he shook his head. "Not that I know of, he was breathing when I left him in the alley. But who knows, he was in really bad shape so maybe he didn't make it out of that rank shithole."

John gave him a single nod before sitting heavily in a living room chair.

"I need to clean up. Make yourself comfortable, and I'll be right out."

V.A. Dold

Twenty minutes later he pulled a clean T–shirt over his head and powered up his laptop. Jack and Michael had joined John in the living room with a twelve pack of beer.

"Hi, guys. I need to talk to Julia and then we can organize our trip home."

Jack stood, ready for action. "Would you like us to finish the job you started today?"

"No, he's not worth your effort. But thank you for offering."

Jack nodded his acceptance and sat again as Thomas logged into Skype and placed his call.

Thomas saw her breath hitch and her eyes widened. The color drained from her face as her eyes jumped to his.

"Tommy," she whispered and he felt her arms wrap around him through their bond.

His first thought was *Damn; I didn't clean up well enough.* Then he asked, "How did you touch me just now? We haven't been able to do that since I got here."

"I don't know. Maybe it's my intense need to hold you? I've heard extreme emotions can overcome distances sometimes." Julia visibly trembled. "What the devil happened to you? That isn't from training is it?"

"No, baby. This isn't from my training. I had a little meet and greet with my father."

Julia gasped, her hands flying to her mouth in shock.

"Believe me, he's in much worse shape than I am, and he deserved every punishing blow I delivered."

"Oh, cher. I'm so sorry. Are you okay? I can be on the Le Beau jet within the hour."

THOMAS: Le Beau Series

"No, sweetheart. Don't do that. I'm flying home in a few hours. We just need to wait for the sun to set." Then he smiled softly. "I'll have you in my arms in a matter of hours."

Gazing into her concerned eyes, his focus became like tunnel vision, there was no one else in the world. Only Julia. Only her beautiful, smiling face, and soft voice.

She held his gaze as she reached out to touch his bruised and battered face on the monitor as if she would actually feel his warm skin beneath her fingertips. Her palm curved to cup his cheek gently before her fingers followed her gaze down his chest.

"Oh, mon amour. It's so painful to not be with you right now," she cried softly. That statement was the closest she had come to admitting the pain she felt. But in this instance it was pain caused by her inability to cradle him in her arms and soothe his pain.

Only a couple of weeks ago, he would never have talked to a woman so intimately in front of an audience. And when he caught John grinning at him, he knew his little brother was going to have fun teasing him tonight, but he didn't care. Nothing mattered, but the woman gazing at him with love and concern in her eyes. Let him have his fun, in the end, he would have Julia in his arms and John would sleep in an empty bed. A little heckling was a small price to pay for this healing moment. He had the soft eyes and warm heart of the woman he loved, comforting his tattered soul.

Thomas kept her talking until he was satisfied he had calmed her fears. When he was sure she would stay put and wait for him, he said. "I can't wait to see you, babe, and I hate to say goodbye, but I need to pack and get to the helipad."

"Okay, but you take extra good care of yourself. My heart can't handle any more injury to you. To tell the truth, I have to work a few hours tonight, so I should get going, too."

"If you're not at home, I'll come to the bar," Thomas assured her.

"Hurry, cher," Julia whispered as she kissed her fingertips and touched them to his lips on the monitor. "I need to hold you in my arms."

Thomas hesitated for a moment, holding her gaze with his own. Then boldly he said. "I love you, Julia." And ended the call.

Thomas turned his computer chair around to face John and their friends. "Shut it. All of you."

John busted a gut laughing so hard he had tears running down his face.

"Whose going to be laughing tonight when I have a beautiful woman in my arms, and you have a cold empty bed?"

That shut John up faster than a bucket of ice water over his head.

Thought so.

"According to Google, we have one hour until sunset. Let's get packed and hit the helipad in an hour fifteen."

"You got it," Michael said as he and Jack headed out the door.

John offered him a beer and sat quietly sipping his own while Thomas packed.

Thomas knew something was bothering John and waited for him to speak.

THOMAS: Le Beau Series

"Are you okay?" John finally asked. "I know I've wanted to beat the shit out of that bastard for years, but you actually did it."

"I'm fine. I would have killed him, but Hans stopped me."

"Why the hell did he do that!"

"He didn't want me living with the knowledge and guilt of having killed my own father. Regardless of how nasty and worthless he is."

John sat silently for a few minutes before he nodded. "Yeah, I guess I can understand that."

Thomas zipped his suitcase closed and grinned at John. "It was great knocking the piss out of him though."

They made good time during the flight. And now butterflies were tap–dancing a jig in his stomach just thinking about kissing his woman senseless. He cut the motor of his new boat and docked at The Backwater's pier. Finally, he was truly home.

Chapter 11

The bar was packed to the rafters, and the band was rocking the dancers on the hardwood floor. Thomas slipped in unnoticed and managed to grab a table in the back.

The constantly moving crowd made it difficult to keep Julia in sight but when he was able to catch a glimpse, he couldn't take his eyes off her.

Her golden hair was tied back in a messy ponytail. And as she moved behind the bar, the overhead lights occasionally hit the soft tresses just so, showcasing the myriad of blond hues that layered throughout her heavy curtain of hair. His fingers itched to weave their way into all that soft silk. Tonight he had plans to do just that.

The sexy cashmere sweater she wore hugged all her assets. With every move, he got to enjoy the jiggle and sway of her incredible breasts beneath the soft pink sweater. That single thought had him quickly scanning the crowd to make sure none of the men were admiring the assets only he had a right to appreciate.

THOMAS: Le Beau Series

Not a single man was daring to ogle her as she hustled to make another round of drinks. Logan must have let the men know she was off limits while he was away.

That's right, guys, the curvy bombshell behind the bar is all mine.

Julia's head rose, and her eyes searched the bar. Her wolf was on full alert; Tommy was near. He was the only person who could cause such a reaction in her. He was here, somewhere in the bar; she felt him. His energy swirled around her, like a soft caress. Excitement coursed through every fiber of her being, setting her pulse pounding. Sure enough, he was sitting in the shadows, against the far wall, devouring her with his eyes. As she stared back, a woman at the table beside him struggled to pull two of the tables together into a group setting. Julia knew from watching him; Thomas always stepped in to help anyone in need. He would never admit it, but he was always the first person to offer help. He might try to appear grumpy to the world, but on the inside he was all sweet gooey marshmallow. An amazingly good man, one she was proud to call 'mate'.

As she continued to watch, one thing became visibly clear. Her man really filled out his clothes nicely. For just a moment, she wished she were the cotton threads in the t–shirt that he wore like a second skin. A perfectly fitted, very lucky t– shirt. His shoulders rolled, and back muscles rippled as he moved the heavy antique tables into position.

Her wolf rumbled its contentment to have its mate safely home. Just the sight of him made her mouth water. Absentmindedly, she licked her lips, in anticipation of the private moments that she knew were coming in the very near future.

This was the perfect opportunity to sneak up on him. Julia leapt over the bar, easily slipping through the crowd until she stood directly behind him.

He must have sensed her presence. Slowly he turned, his expression instantly shifting from concentration to desire. He stepped into her, trailing his fingers up her bare arms until he reached her face. Leaving a wake of goosebumps over her exposed flesh.

Still holding her gaze, he gave her a wicked grin and whispered, "You might want to close your eyes for this."

"Bring it, mate." She grinned back as she stood on her tiptoes and tilted her head just right to kiss the pants right off him.

The crowd faded away as Julia became the entirety of his world. Much too soon, air became a necessity, forcing Thomas to draw back far enough for them to draw air.

"How long is your shift?" he whispered against her neck. "I really need to taste you."

She had been hot and bothered before, but with his throaty declaration, she was dripping wet now. Her whole body tightened and her nipples became beacons for all to see. On top of that, her wolf wanted to rub her head against his chest.

"You do?" she whispered back.

"Oh, yeah. I really, really do." He moaned, his attention still glued to her mouth and his very hard erection pressed into her belly.

Julia rubbed against him as she licked her lips. "Just one more hour and I'm all yours."

THOMAS: Le Beau Series

If it was possible, his sexy growl made her even hotter.

"As much as I hate to say it, I need to get back behind the bar."

"All right, I'll be right here when you're ready to leave."

*****

A long, low groan rumbled from Tim's throat, every inch of his body ached when he tried to move. What the hell had he done last night? Whatever he'd taken must have been strong shit.

When he tried to squint enough to see where he was, pain shot through his entire face. Slowly and carefully, he tried to open his right eye, but all that earned him was another spike pounded into his brain. Hesitantly, he tried again with his left, expecting another jab of intense pain. Even though, it hurt like a son of a bitch, that eye at least opened to a thin slit allowing him to look around and figure out where the hell he was.

What the hell?

His sight was so severely restricted; he had zero peripheral vision and could only see directly in front of him. It hurt like a son of a bitch to turn his head to see his surroundings, but that was his only choice.

The lump in his pocket was encouraging; at least he still had his cell phone. Once he figured out where he was, he could call an ambulance because he sure as hell wasn't going to be able to walk out of this alley on his own power. He could call 911 as long as his phone wasn't smashed or dead, that is. The condition of his phone was still a mystery since he couldn't get to his pocket. He was jammed behind a dumpster and would need to wiggle his way out before he could reach it to make the damn call.

He had two choices, give up and die, or work his way out of this predicament. Taking a deep breath, he braced his arms to push; this was going to hurt like hell.

It was the longest, most painful hour of his life. Sweating like a pig and panting from the pain he reached for his phone and called for help.

*****

Julia had been pouring drinks at a breakneck pace for the last thirty minutes. The crowd seemed extra thirsty tonight. In between orders, she snuck glances at her personal Mr. Sexy Pants, not in the least bit surprised to find him undressing her with his eyes. She'd felt his gaze since turning her back to return to the bar. She found she really enjoyed being the center of his world. Like, enjoyed it a lot.

Pouring out a line of eight whiskey shots, she gazed back, nibbling her lower lip and doing a little visual undressing of her own.

"If you two don't get out of here, I'm going to puke," Logan snarled playfully from his station at the other end of the bar. "Quintin just came in, he can help close tonight. Grab your mate and leave me in peace."

"You're just jealous," Julia teased. "I can hardly wait until your mate shows up."

"Me, either," Logan mumbled.

Julia waved Quintin over and got him up to speed on the orders that needed to be filled then headed for her office to get her purse. With every step her excitement grew. It was finally going to happen; she was going to get Tommy naked and into her bed.

THOMAS: Le Beau Series

The office door hadn't swung shut when she felt Tommy's arms wrap around her from behind. "You're killing me, woman."

"I just need to get my stuff, and we're out of here."

In a flash they were walking through the back door of her cottage, kicking their shoes off.

Tommy must have come here first. She thought as she took in the flickering candles throughout the house. Then she saw the rose petals trailing down the hall.

She turned to him, a five thousand watt smile lighting her face. "You did all this?"

Thomas gathered her into his arms. "I want our first time to be a memory you hold dear for the rest of your life."

Julia gasped and covered her mouth with a trembling hand, a single tear rolling down her cheek.

"Ah, hell. I'm sorry, babe. Just give me a minute, and I'll clean it all up."

"Don't you dare touch a single thing!"

Thomas frowned at her completely confused.

"But, it made you cry."

"Happy tears," she thumped his chest, "you – you – man."

Thomas ran his fingers through his hair and grinned at her exasperated expression. "I swear, women should come with an owner's manual."

Standing stocking foot, in soft worn jeans and black T–shirt, her sexy man made it difficult to think straight. Julia leaned her forehead against his chest, closed her eyes, then drew in a deep breath, filling her senses with his warm spicy scent. A grin spread across her face. All male – her male.

Slowly she raised her head and kissed him softly before stepping from his arms with a saucy expression on her face.

"I'll be right back. Meet me in the living room."

She disappeared down the hall to her bedroom.

Minutes later she joined him in a sheer robe and barely-there teddy.

The heat in his eyes, as he slowly checked her out from head to toe, could have set her house ablaze. It certainly got her heart pounding. Beating crazy fast, like a snare drum solo.

His lips slowly spread into a smoking hot sexy grin.

"Come here, I need to touch you," he demanded, in a husky voice.

The touch of his hands, as he drew her closer made the butterflies in her stomach, do the rumba.

Thomas pulled her lips to his, tasting and savoring Julia's unique essence. With one hand laced in her hair and the other firmly on her hip, he nestled her between his legs.

Julia melted into him, giving herself over to his magical touch. Their tongues danced a passionate, slow waltz, as her fingers worked the buttons on his shirt.

Blazing a trail of hot kisses across his jaw and down the side of his neck, she pushed the shirt from his shoulders. Stopping only to lave the spot on his neck where she would mark him during the ritual. The contented rumble of her wolf joined their sighs and moans.

Each gentle stroke of Thomas's thumbs across her hardened nipples increased her pulse, making it harder to concentrate on tasting every inch of her mate.

Thomas reclaimed her mouth, kissing her to within

an inch of her life. Vaguely the thought that one night with him and she could die happy flitted through her oxygen starved brain.

Then she teetered over the edge and suddenly tasting every inch of him no longer mattered as much. She would get back to that in a minute. His hands gripped her ass, kneading and slipping under the elastic to stroke her soft skin. He had worked his lips down her neck and was arching her back to suckle her through the teddy.

"This has to go," he said around her engorged nipple before lifting his head.

After thirty seconds of steadier breathing, she still couldn't call her heavy panting regular. Not by a long shot, but she was able to string a coherent thought together. Almost.

Had he asked something?

Thomas fingered the silky lingerie. "Babe? This really has to go, and I'm sure you don't want me to go cave man on this sexy bit of nightwear."

With her mind functioning again, she gave him a sexy smile before pushing him back into his chair. Taking two steps back, she began performing a mind–blowing strip tease. Thomas knew if she kept gyrating and, Lord have mercy, bent over again he was going to shame himself before he got his jeans off.

Barely able to speak, he said. "Damn, woman, you're killing me. Take it off and bring your naked self over here."

Julia laughed at his flustered expression as she stepped from the teddy, leaving it lying on the floor as she stepped between his legs, wearing nothing but her high heels.

V.A. Dold

She waited for his eyes to find their way to her face before she reached for his zipper. He lifted up, helping her pull the denim and from his hips.

Commando!

As the jeans passed his feet, she stripped his socks off, too.

Reaching for her again, he slid his hands up her legs, brushing his thumbs over her glistening center. His cock jerked in anticipation of her moist, tight heat. "You're wet for me, babe."

He encouraged her to join him on the chair. "Kneel on either side of me up here on the chair, I need to taste you."

She was a feast at precisely the perfect level. Gripping her hips, he pulled her to his hungry mouth. He breathed her in, before taking one slow lick.

Julia's head fell back as he encouraged her to arch her hips and press against his seeking tongue. He couldn't get enough, licking and sucking, in total bliss. She was sweet and salty on his tongue.

Julia was getting close, her hips grinding against him, rocking in rhythm to his licks and suckles.

Her body stiffened, and she shouted his name as he greedily lapped up her orgasm.

Gripping her hips to steady her quivering body, Thomas lowered her to sit on his bare lap. Straddling him, her heated core slick with her release, slid up and down his aching erection.

This chair was his new favorite piece of furniture. First her heat was in the perfect position, and now her luscious breasts were before his lips begging for his attention. Closing his eyes, he groaned in pleasure as he ran his tongue around her puckered nipple. Each pull on her rosy peaks had her wriggling in his lap. The most wonderful torment he could imagine.

As much as he was enjoying himself, he wasn't going to last. "Baby, I need you. Ride me, mon amour."

Julia lifted enough to wrap her fist around his straining cock. Claiming his lips, she kissed him hard and deep, stroking him from head to balls, over and over. His breathing became ragged, and his head was spinning. One last stroke and she held him in place as she lowered onto him. Taking everything he had.

"Yes…" Her throaty cry mingled with his satisfied groan.

"Ah, hell yeah. You feel…perfect," he growled, voice husky and deliciously hot.

Thomas's head fell back as she rode him like she was a cowgirl, and he was her favorite pony. Gripping his shoulders she lifted slightly with each stroke before taking all of him again. Rocking faster and harder. They were both so worked up; it didn't take long for them to peak. Julia cried his name again as Thomas yelled hers in return.

Gasping for breath, she collapsed against his chest. Thomas held her, stroking her back and hair, wearing the biggest, sappiest grin he was sure he had ever worn. Except for the fact that they were naked, he wouldn't have cared if the whole world saw how happy he was.

Finally able to breathe normally, Julia raised her head. Instantly she saw the bruising and contusions she hadn't noticed in the heat of their passion. A distressed cry broke from her throat. Her lips trailed down the side of his face, and across the bluish purple bruising over his ribcage. Kissing him all better.

How bad is it? Her fingers gently skimmed near a particularly ugly contusion. *Please don't sugarcoat it.* There was desperation in her thoughts and Lord help him—tears running down her face.

His chest tightened. How the hell did men survive a woman's tears? Again, where was the owner's manual when he needed it?

Baby, please don't cry.

He framed her face with his battle-torn hands. Bloodied knuckles and swollen fingers stood out like ugly disfigurements against her creamy smooth skin. He hadn't taken the time to see Mom and Grandma for a healing. His focus had been on getting to Julia.

Gently, he wiped her tears away, the pads of his fingers, brushing her lips. The lips of the only woman in existence, other than his Mother or Grandmother, he would die to protect. The woman who could make his heart sore with a smile. Whose kiss took him to paradise. The only woman he would ever love. She was a damned miracle, and it killed him to cause her worry.

"After Las Vegas, I just wanted to come home. You, Julia, are home for me. Would it help if I told you I plan to see the healers in the morning? I love you, baby. Tell me what I can do to make you smile?"

He willingly stripped himself emotionally bare for her. Giving her his heart, and trusting her to hold it gently.

"I'm your home?" she sniffled.

"One hundred percent."

She searched his eyes, and he saw love and delighted surprise, mixed with something so sexy he lifted her from his lap, took her by the hand and ran with her to the bedroom. If he didn't get her to a bed in the next five seconds, he was going to throw her on the floor in the living room and bury himself deep all over again.

*****

What a way to wake up! As Thomas opened his eyes, he looked directly into Julia's beautiful brown gaze. She was draped across his chest, her chin on her arm, watching him sleep and waiting for him to wake.

"Bonjour, mon amour."

It was a good thing he was lying down, Julia's sweet smile, and sexy greeting had his manhood saying good morning in its own special way. Which left little blood for his brain, or balance, heck there wasn't blood for anything else in his body as far as he could tell.

She adjusted her position so she could kiss his already muddled brain senseless.

He could definitely get used to this.

She gave him one last soft kiss and whispered. "I'll meet you in the kitchen. You can tell me what happened in Las Vegas over coffee."

Silently he groaned, as only a man denied can groan. That was not the path his thoughts and body had been traveling down.

He threw his arm across his eyes and willed his Johnson to relax. Not as easy as it sounded. He owed her an explanation of what happened and how he came to be the bruised mess he was. If the tables were turned he sure as hell would demand one from her, so he would man up and find his damn pants. How do jeans disappear? It took a minute, but the AWOL jeans were located under his new favorite chair in the living room. It baffled him how they had gotten there, but then again, last night had been very –active.

Julia handed him a huge steaming mug. Nothing, except Julia that is, smelled as good as fresh coffee in the morning.

"Would you like to sit here in the kitchen or get comfortable in the living room?" Julia asked as she looked at him over the rim of her coffee with vanilla creamer.

"Here at the table is good. Closer to the coffee pot." He chuckled, trying to lighten the mood.

He pulled her chair for her and slid into the other at her bistro style table.

"Where to begin? I'm not sure how bad your childhood was with your crazy ass mother, but I hope you'll be able to understand how bad it got for us. Growing up with that bastard was like living in a war zone. We were always on guard. I had escape routes and survival bugout packs stashed in several hiding spots. John and I had secret words and bird calls we used to communicate."

Julia took his hand, offering him her strength through their physical connection.

He searched for a way to explain to her how it had been. Having to describe his childhood and talk about their survival techniques was new to him.

"I tried many times to figure out what triggered my fathers attacks. I thought if I knew what set him off, I could make sure we didn't accidentally provoke him. It was years before I realized there were no triggers; he was just a mean bastard who enjoyed tormenting his children."

Julia didn't say a word, she seem to understand he needed to get this all out without interruption.

"I was ten when he hit me the first time. Before

that, emotional abuse was enough to satisfy him. But for some reason, the older we got, the more physical he became. I knew if I didn't get John out of sight when he was around, he would get slapped around like I had. I started watching hunting shows and reading every survival book I could get my hands on. I had to keep him safe. We never knew when he would show up, so we avoided friendships with the kids at school. We couldn't chance one of them being at our house or coming over to play when he was around. We developed a habit of not allowing anyone outside our little family too close. It wasn't safe, and after a while it was normal for us to live like that. Our dysfunctional way of survival is why neither John nor I ever had a steady girlfriend."

Thomas stared at something over her shoulder like he was watching his childhood play out on the wall behind her.

"Luckily, that was about the same time he stopped coming home. We rarely saw him, but when he did come around, I would hustle John out. We would hide out in a cave I had fortified with bedding, clothing, water, food, everything we would need to stay for days. I kept binoculars in my bug out pack so I could watch the house. We took turns as look out, and as soon as his car drove off, we returned so mom knew we were okay.

"He never physically touched her, not until the huge fight they had in the hotel after she met Cade. Did you know she knocked him out cold?"

"I heard that, but I wasn't sure if it was true or a rumor."

"Oh, it's true. He threatened Cade's life and Mom opened a can of whoop-ass on him. God, I wish I had been there to see it."

Julia giggled; his blissful expression was comical.

"If she had been in danger physically from him, I would never have left her alone at the house. But, for some reason, I don't know why, maybe he knew he couldn't take her. But he left her alone. I think that was his way of tormenting her, through loneliness. Well, that and his blatant affairs. He didn't try to hide them from her and even seemed to do things to make sure she knew about them. I'm ashamed to admit, a man such as that is my father."

Julia brushed her thumb back and forth across the back of his hand. Giving what little comfort she could.

"My mother is an extraordinary woman. There aren't many like her, and the world needs her in it. I would have done anything to protect her and John. I still will. For some reason, she thought it was best for us to stay a family until we were grown. My guess is it was her religious upbringing. As misguided as it was, she stayed for us and tried to give us a happy childhood in spite of my old man. She told me after we moved here that she realized how horribly wrong she had been and begged both my and John's forgiveness. I NEVER want to see my mother that devastated again."

Thomas looked Julia in the eye and held her gaze, his expression fierce.

"I will kill that piece of shit before I ever let him lay a hand on anyone I love ever again."

Julia pulled him into her arms and held him. The emotions raging through him were so intense he shook from them.

"I'm so sorry," she whispered into his ear. "That was a horrible way to grow up, Thomas. But cutting yourself off from meaningful relationships, that takes its toll too. I'm glad he can't affect you – no, control you, anymore. I think what happened to you growing up, your passionate desire to protect others, influenced you to be a police officer." A funny look flitted across Julia's face. "And, as selfish as it sounds, I'm happy I'm the only woman you've ever had feelings for."

He leaned forward, wrapped his hand around the nape of her neck and drew her in for a heart–stopping kiss. "I'm happy you're the only woman too."

"So, what happened in Las Vegas?"

"John and I were coming out of a club." Thomas shuddered as he recalled the stripper that looked like Julia shaking everything her mother gave her on stage.

"Any way, I saw Tim, my father, manhandling a woman young enough to be my sister. To make a long story short, I made him let her go and beat the shit out of him."

"I can't say I'm surprised. After what you told me, you had a lot of years of pent up anger to unleash on him."

"You could say that."

If the streets of Las Vegas didn't end Tim's existence, the day would come when he would have to do it, but he wasn't going to worry her with that. He had better things to do.

"Now, let's talk about happier things. I believe we have a date in the French Quarter today, Miss Le Beau."

Chapter 12

Julia's eyes lit up like fireworks on the Fourth of July.

"I can't tell you how excited I am! I haven't been to the Quarter in ages."

Grinning at her excitement, Thomas chuckled. "Pack your bag and we can head out."

"Pack a bag? Why would I pack a suitcase for a date?"

"I'm taking you to the Quarter for the entire weekend. I arranged it with Logan. The bar staff is covered, and you're all mine until Monday."

Julia trailed her fingers down Thomas's chest seductively. "I had no idea you possessed such mad skills, Mr. James."

"Now stop that, woman." Thomas laughed as he captured her wayward hands. "If you keep that up, we'll never get to the Quarter."

Thomas pulled her close, held her gaze, and growled. "And I have plans."

THOMAS: Le Beau Series

He chuckled as her eyes glazed over. She told him once that he melted her brain and made her forget her own name every time he looked at her like that. Looks like he did it again.

Even though he hadn't planned to court a woman in his lifetime, he had watched his stepfather and uncles closely the past few months. One tip he'd picked up was women loved old– fashioned gallantry. Holding her gaze, he brought her hand to his lips and placed a romantic kiss on her knuckles. From the instant flush of her skin, the burst of fresh snow scent, and shy smile, he knew she liked it. Good, he would definitely be doing that more often. If he knew little else about women, he knew a man needed to both show and tell his woman every day how much he loved her.

Thomas loosened his hold and stepped back. "Now shoo. I can't wait to get you all to myself in the French Quarter."

Julia turned toward the bedroom, giggling when he gave her a little swat on the butt.

It was one in the afternoon, and they were finally on their way. First stop had been Grandma Emma's; he needed the healers to fix his face before taking Julia out in public, and there was no way he was explaining this to his mother in her condition. Grandma and the other healers made quick work of his injuries and as far as anyone would know, he'd never been in a fight. It had gotten so late; they had lunch with Isaac and Emma before they were able to get back on the road.

His heart rate increased every time he glanced her way. He still couldn't believe he was her chosen mate. Taking Julia's hand into his, he was instantly home. Her skin was soft, warm satin under his stroking thumb. It reminded him just how soft the rest of her body had been last night.

She turned her gaze from her passenger side window to look at him.

"Where were you just now?" Thomas asked.

"I got a nasty email from my mother while I was packing. I'm just trying to zen myself into the proper state of mind for our weekend."

"You want me to stop stroking with my thumb?" Thomas asked with a tone of worry in his voice; then his lips tugged into a tentative smile. "I can leave you alone, so you can find your happy place."

She smiled back and shook her head. "No. I found my happy place the minute I saw you at the gathering. Forget my crazy mother; we're going to have an amazing time."

About thirty minutes later, he carefully parked in the spot he had reserved. Visions of Julia's mouth doing magical things to a certain part of his anatomy had been testing not only his driving skills, but also the integrity of the zipper and seams in his jeans.

About fifteen miles back, she had licked her lush lips, then adjusted her v–neck sweater, flashing her generous cleavage. The final straw had been her short skirt riding so far up her thighs he caught a glimpse of red satin panties. No red–blooded male could withstand that!

He pulled the keys from the ignition and turned toward her. The heat in his gaze fried every brain cell she possessed. And when he pulled her face toward him, she forgot her darn name. Again. His kiss was demanding and earth moving. It was wow, just wow!

THOMAS: Le Beau Series

Thomas kissed her lightly one last time before he exited the car and walked to her door to help her out. Taking her hand, he led her to a skinny brick walkway off Dauphine Street between a brick privacy wall and another building.

"Where are you taking me?"

Thomas grinned from ear to ear. "You'll see."

The sidewalk ended at a well–maintained private entrance with five–zero–nine in brass numbers tacked to the forest green wooden door.

Thomas opened the door, keeping his hand on the small of her back as she preceded him into a beautiful, lush garden.

Julia gasped. It was incredible! "What is this place?"

"Our hotel for the weekend. It's called the Audubon Cottages because this is where John Audubon created his bird books."

"No way! How the heck did you find this? There isn't even a name on the door."

"Etienne told me about it." Thomas chuckled. "It seems he was good friends with Audubon back in the day and used to hang out here."

Julia shook her head. "That man gets more interesting every day."

"Good morning, sir. How may I be of service?" the man behind the counter asked.

"Thomas James. I have a reservation for Cottage Two."

"Yes. I see it right here."

They finished the business end of checking in and then the manager grinned happily. "Now that the boring business issues are taken care of let me tell you about this little jewel of the French Quarter. The Audubon Cottages prides itself on transporting its guests back in time to the charm and elegance of old New Orleans. We are your relaxing retreat when you need a break from the energy of the French Quarter.

"We offer many amenities. Your cottage has a private patio with a fountain. Mr. James, this is the key for the fountain. I'm sure you will find it satisfactory. There is a heated saltwater pool and towel and slippers are available poolside. Wi-Fi, of course, breakfast each morning, and in–room kitchenette stocked with complimentary drinks. There is also a Keurig® coffee and tea maker, and the pride of the Audubon, your own butler."

"Holy moly," Julia whispered under her breath.

Thomas just grinned.

"As you can see, there is a large living room and dining table with seating for four. Through this doorway is your king bedroom with large ensuite with a Jacuzzi tub. And the private courtyard is through here. Please, let me know what your needs are, and I will take care of them. Have a wonderful weekend."

"Thank you. It looks perfect," Thomas told him.

The manager gave Thomas a nod and backed out the door.

The instant the manager was out of earshot, Julia rounded on Thomas. "A butler?"

He had to laugh at her expression of disbelief. "Of course, nothing is too good for my lady. If you would like, the butler will unpack your suitcase for you."

"I'm not going to let a complete stranger touch my bras and panties!"

THOMAS: Le Beau Series

He knew his suggestion would get a reaction. And he busted out laughing all over again.

It only took Julia a few minutes to unpack and meet him in the living room. The room was beautiful, hardwood floors covered in an antique rug with a soft suede couch, two matching chairs, and a marble top table for the large flat screen TV. The other end of the space had a round antique dining table with four matching chairs and a kitchenette.

"Are you all set?" Thomas asked.

"All set," she grinned as she snuggled into his open arms.

"I have reservations for dinner at Antoine's at seven, so we have a couple hours. Would you like to take a stroll and browse the shops with me?"

"I'd love to."

He had a plan, thanks to Cade, and he needed to get Julia into Jack Sutton Jewelry to make it happen.

They walked a block and a half down Dauphine Street toward Canal before turning down Conti.

"The Erin Rose bar is just down here on the left side before we reach Bourbon Street. I love their frozen Irish coffee. Would you like one?"

Julia smiled. "That sounds yummy."

They got their frozen coffee and chocolate delight and continued to stroll toward Bourbon Street. It was still early, so the famous party street was fairly quiet. When they reached Bienville Street, Thomas steered them left toward Royal Street.

"I'd like to look at the fine antiques and shops on Royal. I still need to furnish my new house."

V.A. Dold

"Awesome! I love to pick out furniture and decorate! I did the entire Backwater with antiques from the Royal Street dealers."

"Excellent! You can help me because I'm at a total loss."

They were headed toward Rothschild's Antiques when Thomas pointed out Jack Sutton Jewelers. "This is where Cade bought my mom's ring. Let's check it out." Then he chuckled. "You can show me what girls like because like every other man on the planet, I have no clue when it comes to jewelry and my mom's birthday is coming up."

"Oh, okay. I'll help you pick out something."

As they entered the store, Thomas pulled his wallet from his pocket. "I better be ready for when you find the perfect gift for my mom," he joked.

They scanned the displays as they slowly walked through the store. Julia pointed out this and that as they went. When they finally reached the engagement rings, Thomas bent closer choosing a large round solitaire.

"That's pretty, don't you think?"

"A lot of women like those huge diamonds in a high setting that stands about a quarter inch above their finger but I think they snag everything."

"Really?" Thomas folded his arms across his chest and casually challenged her. "I hadn't even thought of that. So in your opinion what is the perfect ring?"

Julia scanned the entire case then moved on to the next. Thomas began to panic; he needed her to pick a ring, and she was walking away from the bridal sets.

That's when he heard a small gasp and her hand went to her heart. "This one," she exclaimed triumphantly as she pointed to a wide intricately engraved platinum band with one karat of pave set diamond around the edges.

Not in a million years would he have guessed she would choose that ring. Not that it wasn't stunning; it just wasn't what he thought of as a normal engagement ring. But then, Julia was just as unique as that ring. So after thinking about it, yeah, it was perfect. Now he had to get her to try it on.

Thomas squinted at it again, making a show of doubt over her choice. Finally, he looked at her with a frown on his face. "Are you sure? It doesn't look like much."

"Let me show you. Ma'am, may I try this ring?"

The sales lady unlocked the case and pulled the ring from the display. "It's a lovely ring. We have had a few in by this designer, but I think this is the most stunning we have had to date."

Julia slid it on her ring finger and thank God, it fit perfectly. He had been sweating bullets for a minute; he knew a ring that wide wasn't the kind of thing the store could resize.

"See," she wiggled her finger at him. "It's perfect," she said almost reverently.

It was a good five minutes before she slid the ring off and reluctantly gave it back to the sales lady. As soon as she moved a few cases down to continue their search for a gift, Thomas slid his credit card to the sales lady. Julia didn't know it, but he had called ahead and arranged the sale before they left her house.

After a few more minutes of shopping, Thomas said. "I do not see anything here. Maybe we can find something in one of the antique shops for her house?"

"Okay, that sounds like a good idea."

V.A. Dold

Thomas let Julia precede him out the door and winked at the sales lady as she stealthily slid him the credit card and velvet box. Now he could breathe a little easier and enjoy the rest of their shopping and dinner.

*****

Two hours later, he held Antoine's door open for Julia. The dinner he had planned was going to be spectacular.

"May I help you?" the maître d' asked.

"Reservation for James," Thomas said in his most authoritative voice.

"Yes, Mr. James. I have a private table waiting for you."

Thomas held the chair for Julia, before leaning forward to whisper in her ear, "You're the most beautiful woman in the entire Quarter tonight."

Julia bowed her head before whispering, "Thank you."

He took his seat and reached for her hand.

Moments later a waiter walked to their table. "Good evening, I'm Reginald and it's my pleasure to serve you tonight. I understand you pre–ordered the five course meal we have created to celebrate our one hundred seventy-fifth anniversary, an excellent choice. The first course is Pommes de Terre Souffles, which is Antoine's classic fried puff potatoes. That is followed by our Appetizer en Trois–a trio of Shrimp Remoulade, Lump Crabmeat Ravigote, and Oysters Rockefeller. The third course is Gumbo Creole. A rich Louisiana gumbo with blue crab, gulf shrimp, and oysters." Reginald paused for a moment to take a leather order pad from his pocket. "For the last two courses you each have your choice of

166

THOMAS: Le Beau Series

Filet de Boeuf avec sauce Marchand de Vin et les champignons – that's fancy for grilled center cut of beef tenderloin topped with Antoine's Marchand de Vin sauce and mushrooms. Or Pompano Ponchartrain, which is grilled filet of Pompano with lump crabmeat sautéed in butter." Reginald looked at Thomas for his answer.

"We will both take the beef tenderloin," Thomas confidently answered. He knew Julia preferred beef to fish.

"Very good, sir. Lastly is dessert. You each have the choice of Meringue Glacee au Chocolate – which is French vanilla ice cream on a lightly toasted meringue shell draped with chocolate fudge sauce. Or Pudding de Pain de Noix de Pecan – a cinnamon and raisin bread pudding topped with a caramel rum sauce."

Thomas looked at Julia for her choice; this was the only course he hadn't been sure of.

"The bread pudding sounds incredible."

"Two bread puddings then," Thomas agreed with a satisfied smile.

"Perfect. Would you like wine or cocktails with dinner tonight?" Reginald asked.

"Would you like a bottle of Merlot?" Thomas asked Julia.

"That sounds great."

"Excellent. I will let the chef know what your choices are and get a Merlot from the cellar."

Julia sat back and giggled once Reginald left the room. "That sounds like a lot of food, but it all sounded amazing. You made an exceptional choice, Tommy."

"Thank you." Thomas was pleased Julia approved of his dinner plans.

Julia smiled and laughed through the entire meal. Thomas was charming and gallant and funny as all get-out. She couldn't have imagined a more perfect date.

Dessert arrived, and though it looked and smelled amazing, she wasn't sure she would be able to eat another bite.

"Will you be disappointed if I can't eat my bread pudding?"

"Absolutely not. I'm not sure I can eat mine either," he chuckled. "I'm going to give it a taste and then throw in the towel."

"Good idea."

Thomas couldn't take his eyes from her as her lips wrapped around the fork full of dripping bread pudding. He watched her eyes flutter shut and her tongue dart out to lick her lips before she chewed daintily. The sexy rumble of satisfaction that came from across the table fluttered over his skin like a lover's fingers, stirring his already aroused body further. His eyes fixed on her caramel rum sauce coated lips as she licked them clean. Already tight slacks became unbearable, imagining Julia giving him that kind of personal attention behind closed doors.

There was no way he was going to last if she took another bite. Thomas signaled the waiter for the bill and ten minutes later; they were strolling hand in hand down Royal Street. Albeit, a little slower than before.

"My next surprise is a bit tongue in cheek." He chuckled with a twinkle in his eyes.

"Really? And what would that be?"

"I booked the eight thirty vampire tour; I wanted the full French Quarter experience." He laughed. "But please don't tell Etienne, I'd never hear the end of it."

THOMAS: Le Beau Series

"This should be interesting." Julia laughed, shaking her head. "I'm curious as to how much they get right."

*****

Thirty minutes into the walking tour, they passed Jack and Michael outside a popular Bourbon Street club. Michael doubled over laughing, and Jack clicked his heels together as he saluted Thomas. Julia giggled while he rolled his eyes. Man, he was going to hear about this one.

It was difficult containing his chuckles and harrumphs as the tour guide spouted one ridiculous, so called, fact after another. Julia solved the problem by hiding her grin behind her hand or burying her face in his chest while her shoulders shook with silent giggles.

If nothing else, it was entertaining and kept his woman in his arms for two hours straight.

Checking his watch, Thomas breathed a sigh of relief. There was only about five minutes left of this sham of vampire facts, and he was in the clear. But he didn't possess that kind of luck.

As the tour group rounded a corner to walk another block, he ran smack dab into Etienne's chest. The regal vampire king raised an eyebrow and cleared his throat as Thomas regained his footing.

"Julia. Thomas. Fancy meeting you here."

"Um... hi, Etienne."

The tour guide slowed the group, but Thomas waved him on. They were done anyway.

Etienne smoothed the lapels Thomas had wrinkled when he caught himself from falling. "Interesting choice of entertainment."

V.A. Dold

"I thought it would be amusing." Thomas grinned as Etienne continued to perfect his appearance.

"Yes. They never get a single thing right."

This comment took Julia by surprise. "How would you know that?"

"It's prudent to stay on top of what the humans know, or think they know, about any of the supernaturals that exist. I, or one of my family, attend the tours on a regular basis."

Thomas nodded, once again impressed by the astute vampire. "Much like Men in Black following the gossip magazines for alien stories."

Completely out of character, Etienne barked out a laugh. "I suppose it is. That is one of my favorite movies, actually."

"Really?" Julia asked. "I have it on Blu–ray, you should come over one night for dinner and a movie."

Etienne gave her a regal nod. "I would love to."

Thomas indicated the Preservation Hall, the famous jazz bar, three doors down. "I was just going to ask Julia if she wanted a night cap. Would you like to join us?"

"On any other night I would be honored, but I can tell this is an important weekend for you, and thus I will give you your privacy."

Thomas shook his head, none too surprised by Etienne's abilities. "Sometimes you are a very scary man."

"You have no idea," Etienne grinned.

They said goodnight and enjoyed a cocktail along with incredible jazz while Etienne monitored the action on Bourbon Street.

THOMAS: Le Beau Series

It was two a.m. when they reached the cottage. Thomas watched Julia yawn as she took a nightgown from the dresser drawer and exhausted, sat on the end of the bed too tired to put it on. Quietly, he joined her, wrapping his arms around her. "I had a fabulous night, and I want nothing more than to sleep with you snuggled against my chest."

Gently, he took the nightgown from her and helped her remove her clothes and pull it over her head. Once she was settled under the covers, he stripped to his boxers and joined her, pulling her close for a sweet kiss before falling to sleep with her in his arms.

Julia woke wrapped in her mate's strong arms. She couldn't imagine a better way to greet the morning.

Sensing she was finally awake, Thomas tightened his hold. He had watched her sleep peacefully, for the past twenty minutes. Happy to just hold her warm, soft curves in his bed.

"Good morning, gorgeous," he whispered into her hair.

"Mmmm." She stretched and raised her face for a proper kiss. "What do you have planned for us today? And why are you dressed?"

"I've been up for a while making coffee. Get dressed and meet me on the patio. I ordered breakfast, and it should be here in a few minutes."

"Excellent, I could use a strong cup of coffee." She kissed him again before pulling the nightgown over her head and dropping it at his feet to walk to the bathroom. She was naked as the day she was born, and with a little

V.A. Dold

extra sway to her hips. She knew he was watching and made sure to give him something to think about after the door was closed.

Thomas swallowed hard, and adjusted his jeans so he could manage to walk to the patio without injuring himself. The woman was going to be the end of him, at the very least she might land him in the emergency room with an embarrassing injury. He stood and eyed the dresser for a moment; maybe he should change into his running pants before they left for the day.

Thomas was sipping coffee at the bistro table on their private patio when she finished showering. Chewing on her lower lip, she toyed with her towel. Private as it was, she still better put some clothes on. Sighing, she rummaged through her drawer for the sexy red bra and panty set she bought specifically for the red halter sundress she planned on wearing today.

This ought to knock his socks off.
What are you up to, you little minx?
You'll see.

Thomas groaned in her mind, making her giggle out loud.

Get your sexy ass out here before the food goes cold.

Seconds later, Julia stepped through the door and sucked the breath from his lungs. "Damn, girl! I can't take you out in public looking that hot. I'll be beating men off you all day."

"I guess you better eat a good breakfast then because you're going to need the energy."

Thomas grabbed her around the waist and hauled her into his lap when she tried to slide past him to the other chair. Brushing his lips over the pounding pulse in her neck, he growled. "Maybe I need to hold you hostage in the cottage for the rest of the day?"

Julia tilted her head to give him better access. "Mmm, tempting."

Thomas lifted his head and kissed her silly. "I better let you eat before the eggs get cold. Cold scrambled eggs are nasty."

With breakfast finished, they relaxed near the fountain, sipping coffee. Julia tilted her head this way and that as she studied the interesting stone face spouting a stream of water from its mouth. Heavy foliage obscured part of the face, making it hard to tell what it was. The fountain was very calming with water spilling into a small basin before draining somewhere she couldn't see.

"I think it's supposed to be a forest sprite."

"Excuse me?"

"A forest sprite. They are little fairies, brilliantly colored, and about the size of a large insect. They have glistening wings and are often confused with exotic insects or flowers unless you look closely and know what you're looking for. I have quite a few near my house."

Thomas listened to her, shocked and yet not surprised to learn of yet another supernatural being. "You'll have to show me sometime."

"Oh, sure," she said like it wasn't unusual to discuss the existence of fairies. "They usually come around in the evening right before dusk."

She set her empty coffee cup down and reached for the carafe. Dang, it was empty.

"Want some more? We can stop at Café Beignet on Royal?"

"That sounds great!"

V.A. Dold

It was a short five–minute walk from their cottage to Café Beignet. The coffee shop was one of his favorites, sitting alongside the Police station and practically across the street from the condo the Le Beau's owned. No one lived in it at the moment; it was more of a getaway for the family when they needed it. That, and when one of the Le Beaus came home who didn't have a house built yet, sometimes they stayed in the condo instead of at the main house with Mom and Dad. Regardless, no one outside the main family knew about the condo, and they wanted to keep it that way. Otherwise, he would have used it this weekend.

Lady luck was on his side; there was one open table on the patio. He loved to sit under the shade trees on the patio and people watch. He never knew what was going to walk, roll, or stumble by, but it was a kick watching it happen.

"We didn't find a gift for Mom yesterday and we still need a ton of furniture for the house. Want to shop for a couple hours? We don't need to be to the landing at the river until about two."

Dang it. He hoped she hadn't caught the slip about them needing furniture for 'their' house.

"Sure, when I'm finished, we can get a refill for the road."

Whew, that was close.

*****

Several hours later, he had a new dining room set on its way to their house, and a stunning antique patio set for his mother. Shopping had never been so fun, and Julia made all the difference.

THOMAS: Le Beau Series

"Okay, big guy. Want to tell me what happens at two o'clock?"

"I got us tickets on the Steamboat Natchez for the afternoon Jazz cruise. I hope that's okay with you?"

Julia made a high–pitched squee and jumped up and down like a five–year–old. "I've always wanted to do that!"

Thomas laughed at her antics. "Good, I'm glad you're excited. The cruise is from two thirty to four thirty, and then I have plans for you at the cottage."

Julia watched his eyes dilate with passion at the mention of the cottage and his plans. *I wonder what he's up to?*

They found a comfortable spot along the railing where they could see everything and hear the guide pointing out landmarks and telling fascinating stories of long ago.

The past two hours with Julia in his arms along the railing had been heaven. Thomas removed his arms from around her and took her hand so they could exit the riverboat. He thought he knew a lot about New Orleans, but the rich history he learned during the cruise made him itch to do a little more research into its past. But for now, he had a big night ahead of him, and Julia was going to have his undivided attention.

❧❧❧❧❧

Chapter 13

Thomas closed the door of their cottage and pulled the love of his life into his arms. Breathing in a lung full of her fresh wintery scent, he moaned as his groin tightened. Julia slid her palms up his chest and around his neck, pulling him in for a heart–stopping kiss.

He pressed his forehead to hers. "I need you so badly, but I have very important plans for you. As much as I want to strip that sexy dress off your incredible body, getting you naked will have to wait a little longer."

Her eyes twinkled with curiosity. "What exactly do you have planned?"

"That's a surprise. If you need to freshen up before dinner, I can wait a few more minutes."

Julia frowned at him playfully before she went to freshen up. Goddess only knew what he had up his sleeve this time.

A few minutes later, she joined him in the living room ready for yet another surprise. The more time she spent with Tommy, the more he amazed her with his thoughtfulness.

THOMAS: Le Beau Series

"Ready?" he asked with a knowing grin tugging his lips.

"As ready as I can be. Am I dressed okay?"

"Perfectly." He winked as he took her hand and led her to the end of the private patio only to stop in front of the fountain.

Julia cleared her throat. "Um...what are you doing?"

He answered with a smile as he pulled an extremely old key from his pocket. Using his left hand, he swept some of the vines aside to show a hidden keyhole. A half turn of the key caused the fountain to swing slowly open presenting them with a sweeping staircase.

Julia gasped and gripped his arm tightly. The arc of the stairs hid their final destination from her view, and the excitement of discovering what was up there had her heart pounding.

"Cover your eyes and I will lead you up the stairs. I don't want you to see it until we reach the top."

Julia chewed her lower lip and covered her eyes. She felt Tommy take her arm and gently show her the first stair before leading her slowly and carefully up the ancient stone steps.

"Okay, you can look now." Thomas held his breath waiting for her reaction.

"Oh, my. This is amazing!"

She stood before a secret garden, hidden in the middle of the city. A beautiful table was set with a linen cloth and candles. Rose petals and tiny candles floated on the surface of an identical fountain to the one they had passed through to get here. The China was gorgeous. As she walked to take a closer look, she recognized it as a set she had admired in one of the shops yesterday. Movement off to the side caught her eye as a woman stepped into view holding a violin and began to play softly.

"When did you do all this?" she breathed in awe.

"The butler here comes in very handy. I described what I wanted, and he arranged everything, down to the meal that will be served."

Julia turned to him and pulled his lips to hers for an emotional kiss. "Oh, Tommy, thank you."

"I would move heaven and earth for you, Julia," he said softly, caressing her cheek. "There is nothing I wouldn't do for you."

Julia turned her cheek fully into his palm, closed her eyes and committed this moment to memory. When she opened them, a twinkle in one of the gardens trees caught her eye. A second later, another twinkle flickered a few inches from the first.

"Of course," she whispered and grinned at him. Taking his hand, she pulled him to the tree. "Stay very quiet and try not to make any sudden moves."

He wasn't sure what she was doing, but followed her instructions. He watched as she slowly held her hand out below a thickly leaved branch of the tree. For a few seconds nothing happened, but then he saw it, a glimmer. What looked like a large insect timidly stepped from the leaves into her palm. A tree faerie!

"You can step closer now, but move slowly. They're very skittish," she whispered.

Thomas moved as slowly as he could until he was beside her. The tiny faerie was beautiful! Blinking huge blue eyes, it looked as interested in him as he was in it.

Carefully, Julia lifted her palm toward the tree so the faerie could step back into the cover of the leaves.

THOMAS: Le Beau Series

Thomas leaned close to her ear and whispered. "That was remarkable!"

"They are very curious and mischievous creatures. I sometimes sit for hours and watch them from my back deck."

Thomas took her hand, and they walked back to the table. He helped Julia with her chair before taking his own. A bottle of red wine was already breathing in the center of the table and ready to be poured.

"Would you like a glass?" he asked as he held the bottle slightly tipped.

"Yes, please."

Thomas filled hers and then his own. Raising his glass, he said, "To the most beautiful woman in the world and the man lucky enough to claim her as his mate."

Julia raised her glass and sipped to his toast. As the delicious wine hit the back of her throat, she sputtered. Setting the glass down with a trembling hand she asked, "What did you just say?"

Thomas gazed into her eyes as he took her hand.

"I've never shared my heart with any woman. There's never been any desire to take that chance. But with you Julia, I want to do just that. I really want to take that chance."

Julia gripped his hands tighter. "Really?"

Thomas gave her one of his rare, heart-stopping smiles. "Absolutely. My heart belongs to you, completely."

Thomas slid from his chair and went to one knee.

"Julia." There was a raw love in his voice. Hunger. Yearning.

V.A. Dold

There was one thing he was absolutely sure of; he would never want another woman the way he wanted his mate. She was his end all–be all.

"Calendar–wise, I only met you a few weeks ago. But in here," he thumped his chest, "in my heart and soul, I've always known you. You're the only person I've trusted enough to see me. The real me. I've let you into places; no one has ever been allowed or ever will be again. And despite that, God only knows why, you still want me and love me."

She parted her lips to speak, but he stopped her with one gentle finger on her lips.

Opening the little velvet box to display the platinum band she had chosen at Jack Sutton Jewelers, he asked. "Julia Le Beau, will you be my wife and also complete the ritual with me. Right here in our cottage. Tonight?"

Her lip began to quiver as she whispered. "Yes, Tommy. Oh, yes. I will be your wife! And I've been waiting to complete the ritual with you."

Thomas took his seat again holding her left hand with his right. The ring shimmered in the soft glow of the candles, looking perfect on her finger.

They both turned toward the tree as a golden light twinkled across the garden and floated to the table beside their hands. His shocked eyes shot from the golden and silver faerie with an iridescent crown to Julia. She was staring at the beautiful creature with a look of amazement on her face as well.

The faerie blinked up at him before she gently touched his hand with her left hand then she blinked at Julia and touched her hand with her tiny right hand. In a tiny, high–pitched voice she said, "Julia has been a good friend and ally to my people. I bless this union with a layer of faerie protection. No creature, human or supernatural, will ever be able to come between you. May you experience the love you both deserve and be blessed with many healthy children."

Then, the faerie touched Julia's ring. Instantly it glowed as if lit from inside and the tiny diamonds around the edge sparkled rainbows all around them. "If you are ever in need of me, touch this ring and call me. I will come instantly to your aid."

With a regal nod to each of them, she rose in the air and shot like a shooting star back to the tree.

Thomas stared at Julia with his mouth hanging open. "Was she the faerie queen?"

Julia nodded, still speechless. Finally, she said. "I've heard of her existence, but I have never heard anyone tell of meeting her. Not even Etienne." Her eyes grew larger, and she drew in a little gasp. "A blessing from her is highly prized. You have no idea how powerful she is. With a snap of her fingers, she could level this entire city."

Thomas sat back in his chair, staring at her as he absorbed what she just said. Then, slowly his gazed moved to the tree, and as if to answer his unspoken question a golden light twinkled once.

"Holy, shit!"

"You could say that again." Julia nodded.

Slowly the glow subsided until it appeared to be like any other ring. No one would ever be able to tell it was a direct link to the faerie queen.

Before either of them had time to say more, the butler pushed a serving cart toward the table. "Would you like the meal served now, sir?"

V.A. Dold

Thomas frowned as if making a decision. Then he turned a questioning gaze to Julia and raised an eyebrow.

Are you hungry – for food?

Not really. With all the excitement, I'm not sure I can eat. Sorry.

No need to apologize, babe. My appetite is for other things at the moment.

His eyes grew dark with hunger for his mate. Thomas turned his attention back to the butler. "Please, put the dinners into to–go boxes. Thank you for everything you arranged," he took Julia's hands. "The evening was perfect."

Only a few minutes later, they'd gathered the meals, thanked the violinist and were now in the cottage again.

Thomas flipped the lock and spun Julia around trapping her between the door and his raging body. A possessive growl rumbled from his throat, tasting her sweet lips was an all–consuming priority as he lowered his mouth to hers.

Soft moans floated between them, increasing in volume in concert with the heat that was building. Tongues stroked and danced as they memorized each other down to the tiniest detail.

Cupping her face, he tilted her head slightly, and the kiss deepened. Thomas ground his hips into her. Julia's lips were so soft and perfect under his, but he needed more. His cock stiff and throbbing pressed into her soft belly, and his small thrusts turned up the heat until it felt like a sauna. He wanted to cup her breast in his palm and rake his thumb across her nipple, but there wasn't enough space between them for a breath of air.

With more reluctance than he could articulate, he pulled away from her luscious curves and led her by the hand to their bed. With every step, he told himself the results were worth the loss of her in his arms for a few seconds.

His agony ended at the edge of the bed. Julia took his face in her hands and kissed him until his head spun. Then, she put just enough space between them to remove his tie and unbutton his shirt. When Thomas moved to take charge, she tapped his chin with her finger.

"Tommy, tonight I'm in charge." She raised her eyebrows in challenge to make her point.

A grin broke across his face as he kissed her once and said. "I'm more than happy to be at your mercy, babe."

Julia made short work of his clothes, and with a wicked grin pushed him onto the bed. Laughing, Thomas propped himself on his arms to watch his sexy woman strip. Damn, had she taken classes? Because, good Lord, she was smoking hot! When she turned away from him and bent over, wearing nothing but stilettos, he thought he was going to cum without her even touching him.

Julia licked her finger and sucked it suggestively, all while holding his gaze. She pulled her finger from between her lips with a 'pop' and slowly crawled up his painfully aroused body.

Waggling her finger at him she said. "No touching."

She positioned both knees on either side of his hips, her heated, wet core sliding erotically along his engorged erection. Her hands cupped the breasts his mouth was salivating to taste, kneading and pinching her nipples into hard peaks.

"Please, baby. Let me touch you."

Julia simply licked her lips in answer to his plea and rocked slightly harder against his cock to add more friction. The candlelight glowing around the room played over her curves, caressing the swell of her breast. Locking her gaze with his, she rolled his male nipples between her fingers and took one of his hands to her mouth. She separated his index finger from the others and sucked it into her mouth, sucking him off like she had his cock instead.

Thomas couldn't take his eyes from her amazing mouth. "Oh, God, babe. I'm not going to last. Don't I need to save that for the ritual?"

Julia gave him a slight pout and released his finger from its hot, wet heaven. Her breathing became ragged, and she finally led one of his hands to her clit. "Touch me, Tommy. Make me cum."

"Hell, yeah." FINALLY!

Seconds later, she screamed his name and shattered beautifully for him.

Julia lay panting on his chest, right where he wanted her. "Kiss me, sweetheart, I need your lips."

She gave him a satisfied smile and offered her lips to him. Thomas devoured her mouth, putting every ounce of sexual tension raging in his body into his kiss. He grabbed her ass and pulled her up his body, stopping to suckle and lick her nipples until she was moaning.

"Grab the headboard, babe, and straddle my face, I have to taste you."

Julia was all for that suggestion. A long low rumble of pleasure rolled from her chest as her wolf voiced its satisfaction.

Thomas had a magical mouth and tongue. He licked and sucked her into the stratosphere. In minutes, he had her shouting his name a second time.

THOMAS: Le Beau Series

Panting she carefully moved to lie beside him. It wasn't easy when her legs felt like a Gumby dolls. "Give me," she panted hard, "a minute and I will start the ritual."

"Whatever you need, baby." His body hummed in anticipation of making her completely his. For now, he was happy to hold her in his arms, running his fingers up and down her body."

"Babe, did you ask your father how the aging thing works with you already being older than I am?"

Once she was able to speak, she said. "I called him and he told me my age will synchronize with yours. So essentially we'll both continue to look like we are twenty-five, and I won't start to age at my normal nine hundred years. Instead, my body will wait for you to reach nine hundred and then we will start to age together until we reach around fourteen hundred." She ran her fingers through his hair as if studying it. "I've been thinking about the color of your wolf. Based on your hair color, I'm not so sure you'll be brown; I think you will look like a normal wild gray wolf. With the tans, and whites, and grays mixed together in its coat."

"That's cool." He grinned. "I was told that the normal magical powers I'll receive are the ability to dress or undress with a thought, which I think is going to come in very handy. Especially the undressing part."

Julia giggled when he tickled her ribs.

"I'm also really looking forward to the healing ability. In my line of work, being able to heal ten times faster will be a huge asset. The ability to move so rapidly, the human eye can't detect me will be cool but since I deal mostly with supes, it'll just make me as fast as they are. We've already talked telepathically and sent each other caresses and feelings of emotion through our magical connection, so no explanation needed there." Thomas paused with a very serious expression on his face. "I think my additional gift will be an enhancement of the one I already have, which might suck unless it comes with the power to control it better."

Julia nodded. "I think you're right, and the enhanced ability usually comes with ways to control and use it, that you never had before. So, I think you'll really like it."

"Thanks, babe, I needed that. For a second there I was a little apprehensive."

"You're welcome, mon amour," she said caressing his chest."

Thomas slid his hands along her collarbones and up her neck to cup her face. Her chest rumbled as he brought his lips to hers, pausing to envelop himself in her scent. He kissed her gently, easing her lips apart and searching with his tongue in an unhurried exploration. Their tongues reached for each other, dancing and caressing. Their kisses were slower and less frantic than before.

He pulled her over his body again to straddle his hips. Then, trailed his palms down her ribcage and over her soft, round belly to stop and grip her hips. He moaned when her heated core ground against him as he pulled her to his lips again.

Slowly, Julia burned a trail of kisses across his stubbled jaw and down his neck, stopping to give special attention to the spot, which would bear her bite. She traced, licked, and nibbled another trail down his chest.

"Baby, you're so damn sexy. How did I get so lucky?"

THOMAS: Le Beau Series

"You must have really good karma," she teased as she rose to sit up and stroke his shaft along her wet pussy.

He reached up and ran one palm from her neck to her heated core while maintaining a grip on her with the other.

She gasped, arching her back when he began stroking her clit. "I need to start the ritual before we go too far. Are you ready?"

"Absolutely."

Taking a deep breath, she started the ritual words. "Will you give yourself, body and soul, to complete this woman and her wolf?

"Will you unite your life with mine, bond your future with mine, and merge your half of our soul to mine, and in doing so complete the mating ritual?"

Without hesitation he answered. "I will give myself, body and soul, to complete you as a woman and her wolf.

"I will unite my life with yours, bond my future to yours, and merge my half of our soul with yours. I will complete the mating ritual with you."

Julia used her thighs to lift her body off his hips so she could position his erection where she needed it. Never losing eye contact, she sank down onto him until he was seated fully.

Thomas gripped her hips rising to meet each of her rocking thrusts. Their panting grew heavy, and she knew they needed to complete this now.

"I claim you as my mate." The magic began to swirl around them.

"I belong to you as you belong to me.

"I give you my heart and my body.

"I will protect you even with my life.

"I give you all I am.

"I share my half of our soul to complete you.

"I share my magic with you."

Julia leaned forward kissing Tommy deeply before trailing her lips to his neck. She lapped where his shoulder and neck met, once, twice, a third time, and then bit, piercing the flesh with her wolf's canines.

Thomas groaned, he'd heard the bite was erotic, but this was so much more than he had expected. His hips jerked into Julia, slamming his raging cock deep as Julia licked the wound clean.

With one last lick, she began again. "I beseech the great Luna Goddess to bless you and your wolf guardian.

"You are my mate to cherish today and for all time.

"I claim you as my mate."

He felt something like a wind enter his body; it made him feel full and complete. Funny, he'd never felt incomplete before, at least not that he'd noticed. But then, his mother had done everything in her power to make him feel more loved then any of the kids he ever met. As a matter of fact, he'd often felt bad for the other kids who were more ignored than loved by their mothers. Now, it made sense, as a shifter mate she had sensed his need without even knowing she was doing it. Through the fog of his thoughts, he heard Julia's sweet voice.

"Tommy, you need to repeat the words back to me."

He looked directly into her eyes and began. "I claim you as my mate.

"I belong to you as you belong to me.

"I give you my heart and my body.

"I will protect you even with my life.

"I give you all I am.

"I share my half of our soul to complete you."

THOMAS: Le Beau Series

Julia laughed as she felt their souls come together, as if tiny knitting needles rapidly closed the gap between the two halves to leave a complete, glowing soul.

"It tickles." She laughed again.

Thomas chuckled as he continued. "I share my magic with you."

He pulled Julia down to him so he could reach her neck. He copied what she had done, lapping. Once, twice, a third time. Suddenly canines erupted in his mouth. The teeth only stunned him for a moment before instinct took over, and he bit down.

Julia moaned, rocked as best she could, lying on his chest.

He licked the wound clean and said. "I beseech the great Luna Goddess to bless you and your wolf guardian.

"You are my mate to cherish today and for all time.

"I claim you as my mate."

With the ritual words completed, she sat up and rode her new mate like there was no tomorrow.

Thomas was right there with her, thrusting his hips up as she came down, using his grip on her hips to help lift her up and slam her home.

"I can't believe you're mine, really mine. God! You're so tight, you feel so good."

Suddenly she exploded in ecstasy. Her channel clamped down on him as she came hard, screaming his name for a third time tonight.

Thomas followed her immediately with his release, yelling her name with abandon.

Julia collapsed to his chest, allowing him to wrap his arms around her. He held her like that for a minute or two before urging her to cuddle beside him where he could hold her while they slept.

V.A. Dold

Breathing out a contented sigh, Julia cuddled into Thomas's side with one arm across his chest.

She smiled as she felt his lips brush her forehead. Comfort and love washed over her as Tommy used their bond to kiss her goodnight.

Chapter 14

Ten a.m. and they were already pulling up to his new house on the royal plantation. "Don't move," Thomas told Julia as he jumped from the car and ran around to open her door. "Welcome home, mate," he grinned as he helped her from the passenger side.

"Wow! I didn't get to look around the grounds much during the gathering. Your security team prevented anyone from wandering outside the party boundaries, so I missed seeing these new homes. This is awesome!"

"I'm glad you like it. Let me show you around."

Thomas took her by the hand and gave her the grand tour. A kitchen that would make a chef think they'd died and gone to heaven, followed by a huge great room with a pool table and monster size flat screen TV. Then it was off to the bedrooms and wrap around balcony on the second floor.

"Um... Tommy. How many kids are you planning on having?" Julia asked nervously, as she counted six bedrooms.

"One or two, why?"

V.A. Dold

"You have a lot of bedrooms for only a couple kids."

Thomas laughed at her horrified expression. "I wanted extra guest rooms for visitors. As chief of security, I have extra guards for events like the gathering, and when they travel to help me on location, they stay with me."

"Oh," Julia said with an embarrassed smile.

"Don't worry, babe. When we decide to have kids, we will decide how many together."

Julia continued to blush as he ended the tour with the master suite: a huge bedroom, sitting room combination with a massive bathroom that contained a Jacuzzi tub large enough for a small family. The walk–in closet, was bigger than her entire bedroom at her house.

"Wow, this is a great house," she called from inside the closet. "Did you design it yourself?"

"Kind of. I told the architect what I wanted and the general layout, and he drew it up for my approval."

She stepped from the closet and wrapped her arms around his waist. "Your house is perfect."

With a raised eyebrow, Thomas used his index finger to lift her chin until she met his gaze. "Our house. And anything you want to change, let me know and I'll make it happen."

Her warm breath raised goosebumps on the exposed skin of his neck, right over her bite mark. Chills ran down his spine as the temperature in the room suddenly increased. The soft press of her lips to her mating mark was almost his undoing.

"Julia," he whispered, as he claimed her mouth.

A soft moan escaped as she parted her lips for him.

THOMAS: Le Beau Series

He swept his tongue inside. Like lovers who had been together for years, their bodies molded seamlessly. One hand wove into her long hair while the other wrapped around her hip, fitting her closer. There was no mistaking his reaction to her; she could feel it pressing into her stomach.

He ended the kiss and held her close. "I'll never get tired of kissing you."

"I certainly hope not." She laughed, with her eyes shining brightly.

"As much as I would love to strip you bare and lock you in our bedroom for a week, we have to get your stuff from your house while we have daylight."

"I know, but you're just so tempting; I couldn't help enjoying your scent. But you're right, we need to pick up a few things from my house and talk to Logan about The Backwater."

As if in response to her mention of the bar, he stiffened and turned in the direction it lay across the swamp. The claiming had enhanced his gift all right, and now he could sense anger and intent to do harm from miles away. The good news was, at least now he could turn it off or tune it to specific people or locations. Being able to pinpoint his sensitivity was a godsend, or should he say a Goddess send.

"Something is wrong at The Backwater," he turned back to her. "I think you should stay here while I check it out."

"Hell no! That's my bar; I'm going with you."

Thomas studied her determined expression for a second. "All right, but I need to gather a couple of the guys before we go. There's no telling what we'll find."

V.A. Dold

Within minutes, they were speeding toward the bar in two of the family's boats. Thomas and Julia in one, while Lucas and Marcus followed in the other.

*****

Tim paced from the door to his kitchenette and back in his tiny efficiency apartment. He'd been blindly moving back and forth, stewing in a brew of hate and revenge for hours. His ex–wife Anna and piece of shit son Thomas would pay for everything they'd done to him.

Passing by his one and only end table, he snatched the backscratcher he always kept handy. Ever since he'd moved to Las Vegas, he had repeatedly broken out in hives and boils that itched like a mother. Countless doctor appointments and allergy specialist had puzzled over his ailment with no solution in sight.

Fuck it; getting revenge on the family who had turned their backs on him was worth the risk. He pulled his cell phone from his pocket and dialed the casino boss in New Orleans he hadn't spoken to in over a year. If he were careful, he could get some information on Anna and Thomas without ending up at the bottom of the Mississippi River, wearing a pair of cement shoes.

Twenty minutes later, he was in debt to the tune of five thousand dollars in exchange for some very interesting information. It seemed Thomas was involved with a woman whose mother violently disapproved of him. And luck was on his side; the mother was willing to disclose the location of a bar in the middle of the swamp where he could locate not only his son but his ex–wife as well. Exacting his revenge was going to be easier than he thought.

THOMAS: Le Beau Series

Thomas and Julia were still a mile out when an explosion reverberated around them. Smoke and flames shot into the sky from the direction of her bar.

Julia clamped a hand on Thomas's arm. "Was that my bar?"

"I'm not sure. Is The Backwater the only structure in that direction?"

"Other than my house, yeah."

Thomas drew her closer; this was going to be bad.

The instant the boat entered the mouth of the bay where her house and bar were, his entire demeanor changed. His body stiffened, and he slammed down the walls in his mind to block her from his thoughts. He morphed into a man she didn't recognize, one who was cold and frightening. He had no expression on his face at all; his eyes turned hard and dangerous. Thomas, the sheriff, was a man even she with her telekinetic abilities didn't want to meet in a dark alley.

"NO!" Julia wailed. Every window was busted out of her beloved bar, and the door hung awkwardly on its smashed hinges. But that wasn't the worst of it, her house was a smoking heap of rubble. The explosion must have been her house.

"Julia?"

Stunned and in obvious shock, she stared at the wreckage, unhearing and unseeing the men around her.

"Julia, I need you to stay on the boat until we check this out."

The instant the boat was within leaping distance; she was racing down the pier and disappearing from sight behind the bar.

"Julia, damn it! Come back here," Thomas barked.

V.A. Dold

It took two tries to secure the boat to the pier; his hands shook so badly with the terror he was experiencing for her safety.

All three men skidded to a halt as the house came into view. Julia stood on the peak of the rubble in what would have been her living room. Wracking sobs shook her body, and a horrible keening ripped from her throat.

Thomas walked around to the other side hoping to find a safe path to reach his mate. The last thing he wanted was to cause the unstable heap to shift with her on top of it.

Damn it! There was no way to get to her; she would have to come to them.

"Sweetheart, please look at me."

Even though she hadn't looked at him, he saw a flicker of questioning recognition glimmer in her eyes.

"Baby, please. I need you to jump to me.' The debris might shift, and you could be trapped under the unstable rubble."

Slowly, her head turned, but her eyes were still very glazed over. He wasn't sure she was hearing him at all.

Suddenly, she gasped, bent her knees slightly and launched herself to the edge of the forest.

"No," she cried weakly. Her voice containing every ounce of heartbreak she was experiencing. From his angle, Thomas couldn't see what she was looking at. Then a flash of blue and another of purple caught his eye.

Thomas held up his hand like a traffic cop toward Lucas and Marcus. "Guys, don't move and stay very quiet."

"Julia? What do you have in your hand?"

Numbed by grief and shock, her movements were jerky and awkward from her sobs and gasping breath.

THOMAS: Le Beau Series

Thomas inhaled sharply when he finally saw what was cupped in her palm. A tiny iridescent faerie lay broken and dying. The others flittered around Julia's head and shoulders unsure what to do but wanting to help their fallen friend.

In a tiny weak voice the faerie whispered. "I tried to stop the bad men, the swamper shifters who attacked Sir Thomas. I'm sorry, I failed." With one last shuddering breath, the faerie died.

A horrible snarl ripped from Thomas's chest as his wolf tried to take charge.

Julia's eyes grew wide, and her heart hammered frantically in her chest.

Tommy stood behind her, wearing the deadliest most intimidating expression she had ever seen. Raw power poured from him as his wolf howled a challenge into the forest.

A whimper of fear from his mate brought him crashing back to reality. The situation that had created a red haze of fury to rage through him came into focus. There was no way in hell he wanted to cause his mate any further distress, but his behavior was doing just that.

Sucking in a deep calming breath, he shook off the rage so he could be the mate she needed and not the dangerous man who was frightening her.

"I'm so sorry." He reached for her to draw her into his arms. "Please, don't be afraid of me, sweetheart."

"You just put on your tough and ruthless sheriff persona. I've never seen you like that before," her voice quavered, but her gaze met his steadily. "You become a different person, a really–REALLY scary person. I understand why you have to be that way, so don't worry, I was just taken by surprise is all."

"I'm sorry, babe. I didn't mean to scare you."

"They destroyed my home, did who knows what to my bar, and," her shoulders shook with her sobs, "killed Daffi." After several minutes, her wracking sobs became shudders and sniffles.

Thomas didn't say a word, he held her tightly, rubbing his palms up and down her back, trying to be the rock she needed.

With tear reddened eyes, she looked up at him and gave him a faint smile. "I knew you probably needed to be a tough guy to do what you do as the head of security. I was just shocked to see you become that person before my eyes."

"I become someone else? What do I do? I don't understand."

"You slammed your walls down to block me out and shut down all your emotions. It was like you separated yourself from the situation and became cold and unfeeling."

"I deal with horrible men and situations every day. I have to shut myself off from that, or I would become insane or suicidal. That is the only way I know how to cope and not allow my work to effect me." Thomas raked a hand through his hair, a blatant sign of his agitation. "What can I do to make you less afraid of me? I can't lose you, Julia."

Julia cupped his face with her warm palm, brushing away his frown lines. "You won't ever lose me, mate. I knew you were this person. I just was surprised to see it. I know you need to do things to survive and cope, I was just shocked by the unexpected change on top of this." She waved a hand at the destruction that used to be her house. "It isn't anything I can't handle, especially now that I know what to expect."

Lucas and Marcus left them to their private moment. The Backwater needed to be checked for damage. It was obvious there was nothing left of the house to be saved but the bar might be in fairly good shape.

"Shit," Marcus growled, as they got their first look inside.

"Whoever did this will die," Lucas snarled.

Marcus and Lucas wove their way through the destroyed interior of the bar. It was so much worse than it looked from the outside.

"Call the guys. Let's get this cleaned up for Julia." Marcus frowned as he righted a chair. "I hate that she is even going to see it like this."

Neither of them had to turn around to know their cousin had joined them. A strangled cried followed by a muffled whimper broke the silence of the devastation that used to be her home away from home.

Lucas glanced over his shoulder to see Julia wrapped in Thomas's arms, her face buried in his chest.

Marcus spoke quietly to the person on the other end of the phone, organizing the cleanup crew and notifying his parents. Isaac was going to blow his top over this attack on his family. If shifters had done this, and it sounded like they had, the swampers anyway, they would die under shifter law. Julia was not only a royal lady through blood as the king's niece but now she was a princess through her marriage to Thomas, the next queen's son. Royal bloodlines only required the king or queen to be the parent, and Thomas fit the criteria. Even though he didn't broadcast it, he was, in fact, a prince.

Thomas rubbed Julia's back as she got herself under control. How much more could his mate take?

With a deep breath, she straightened her shoulders and gave him a small smile. "Thank you for being here for me."

"I will always be at your side, Julia, never doubt that." Julia stepped from his arms to take a good hard look around the bar. Now that she was less stressed, Thomas took the opportunity to check with his uncles. "Marcus, what's the plan?"

"All the men are coming from the plantation except a few guards for the women who will remain. Julia's brothers are also on their way and a few men who live near the bar. We will have this cleaned up in no time so you can take stock of what we need to get it back in operation."

"Excellent. Thank you for taking care of that."

Thomas took Julia's hand and carefully made his way toward the long cypress bar. "Let's let the men handle the tables and chairs while we check the damage behind here."

Julia nodded even though she was behind his back, and he couldn't see her response. She was still too shell-shocked to speak.

"Ouch!" she bumped her nose hard into his back as he came to an abrupt stop.

Dang, that stings. In less than a second her eyes were watering, and her head was one massive headache.

Thomas spun around at her cry of pain. "Sorry, babe. Are you okay?"

Julia gingerly touched her nose. "I'm fine. It always hurts like a mother when you get your nose bonked. Just ask Logan, I've wacked his a few times."

Marcus and Lucas chuckled across the room.

"He never did know when to leave you alone," Lucas said grinning. "I know Krystal wacked him plenty of times, too."

"He's always had a thick skull," Marcus agreed, shaking his head.

"What's the word behind the bar, Thomas?" Lucas asked as he inspected a busted table.

"It looks like they smashed every bottle in the place and Logan is going to shit when he sees his new frozen drink machine."

"Dang it! He just put that thing together, too," Julia whined.

"Do you have insurance on the place, babe?"

"No," she sighed. "It's too far out. None of the companies wanted anything to do with it."

Just then, Logan came skidding through what was left of the door. "What the hell!"

"Swampers," all three men answered at once.

Logan raked his fingers through his hair, and then his eyes went wild. "Julia, you okay? You weren't here when this happened were you?"

"No," she growled. "If I were, there would be bodies to bury."

"Thank Goddess!" Logan grabbed his sister into his arms. "So, do we know who needs killing yet? Because someone is going to die, I can tell you that, right now."

Thomas shook his head. "All we know is it was swampers."

Julia raised her face from her brother's shoulder. "I know who it was. Well, kind of."

Thomas, Marcus, and Lucas stepped closer. "What do you mean?" Logan asked.

"Daffi, or I mean Daffodil, the tree faerie, said it was the swampers who attacked Thomas. Although I don't really know who they were either, except for Blade. I know that moron."

Marcus cracked his knuckles. "So, we find Blade and then beat the information out of him."

"Sounds like a plan to me," Lucas nodded in agreement.

Thomas cleared his throat and waited for everyone's attention. "As much as I want to beat these guys senseless, first we need to get the bar operational, and then we can go swamper hunting. Isn't that what you called it the other day, Marcus?"

"Yeah." Marcus closed his eyes and took a deep breath as if calming his raging temper. "Okay, you're right. We'll get the bar up and running again, and then gather some men to do the job."

Lucas turned to Thomas. "I think we should get Jack and Michael out here to look over the area for clues with us. Their vampire senses may pick up something we don't. There might be clues, other than smell if we can pick one out of the mess, to help us identify them when we go hunting for the assholes."

"Good idea. I'll give them a call and have them come out here after sunset."

A gasp from the entrance had everyone turning toward the door. The work crew had arrived, but there was no way to truly prepare someone for what they'd walked into.

A hair-raising telepathic growl was heard by everyone the instant Isaac stepped from the pier and saw the pile of debris that had been his niece's home and the damaged bar.

THOMAS: Le Beau Series

"What the hell happened here?" Isaac demanded as he stepped through the door.

What little was known about the attack was explained quickly to everyone so the clean up and repair could get underway.

Removing the busted up chairs and tables went rather quickly, cleaning up the broken glass and sticky liquor took a bit longer. Even the glassware lay shattered to smithereens. Thank Goddess, the structure was still sound, and the band stage was virtually untouched.

Logan stood with his arms crossed as his gaze swept the empty room. "Well, it will take a couple weeks, but we will get it back up and running. I'll order new windows and a door tomorrow. Julia, could you order glassware and a new frozen drink machine? I'm not sure where you got that."

"Sure, I can do that easy enough." She nodded as she rubbed the stiff muscles in her neck. "I can get everything online, and they normally deliver within a week. Do you want to call in the liquor order, Logan, or should I?"

"You're newly mated and now you need to deal with replacing all your house stuff. I'll take care of it; just place the online order and leave the rest to me. Besides, you lovebirds should take a few days for your honeymoon.

Julia hugged her brother tightly. "I love you, and I know this is horrible bad timing and a crappy situation, but I planned to ask you if you would like to buy me out of the bar?"

Logan leaned back so he could see her face. "Are you sure? You love this place."

Julia smiled and squeezed him tighter before stepping back to look him in the eye. "Yes, I'm sure. As Tommy's mate, I'll be living at the plantation, and I really don't want to take a boat to the bar every day and in the dark back home every night."

"Good point, I don't want you driving a boat home every night in the dark either," Logan agreed. "I know I'm going to be the owner after I buy you out, but I still want you okay with the new furniture I purchase. Would you mind if I replaced the broken antique sets with solid wood tables and chairs?"

"Not at all. Make the place your own," Julia said as she slipped out of Logan's arms and into her mates embrace. "Besides, I'll find something else to keep me busy, I'm sure. Who knows, maybe we'll work on giving Cade and Anna their first grandchild."

Chapter 15

Thomas's gaze snapped to hers, as Isaac exclaimed his excitement over the possibility of more babies.

"Did I just hear you right?"

Julia grinned up at him. "I don't know, did you?"

"Are you ready for children?"

"Well, if it happens, I'll welcome them," she purred as she ran a finger down his chest. "And until then, I plan to have a lot of fun practicing."

Whistles, catcalls, and "Get a room" were heard throughout the bar.

"I, for one, would like a great-grandchild," Isaac interjected.

Cade made a 'T' with his hands. "Time out everyone, I would appreciate it if you kept all the talk about babies to yourselves until you're sure. I don't want Anna to get her hopes up and then be disappointed. The doctor said she needs to avoid all stressful situations until the baby is born."

Julia looked contrite. "I'm sorry, I certainly don't want to cause her stress. Please, keep this to yourselves everyone. It's not like we're trying to have a baby, just not preventing it from happening naturally."

Isaac clapped Thomas on the back. "Then I won't be surprised by an announcement sooner rather than later."

Logan whistled to get everyone's attention. "If all this talk of babies is finished, I have some friends coming with boats built for hauling and I could use help getting all the busted up tables and chairs to the pier."

The men were making short work of the last leg of clean up, so Julia took the opportunity to check on her faerie friends.

She stopped short as she rounded the corner of the bar. Lilli, the faerie queen, was standing on a low hanging branch with her arms around the two grieving faeries that had been with Daffodil.

A tear ran down Lilli's cheek as she said. "Please, join us."

Julia knelt, so she was eye level with her three weeping friends. "I'm so sorry," she sniffled. "This is all my fault."

"Why would you say such a thing? Did you blow up your house? I don't think so; an evil group of shifter males did that. And I promise you, they will pay with their lives."

"The men are already organizing a swamper hunt along with a couple vampires to deal with them. Under shifter law, their attack on me alone is a death sentence."

"I understand. I will speak with Isaac. Even though it is his right to mete out their sentence, they killed one of my people as well. I will let the men find the guilty parties, but I want to be present when justice is served."

THOMAS: Le Beau Series

"That sounds only fair," Julia agreed. "I am going to miss Daffi so much. Is there anything I can do for her final rights?"

"Thank you, but no. We have a sacred ritual we will perform during which her body will return to dust and her spirit will return to the afterworld to await reincarnation."

Julia nodded and would have spoken again, but voices grew near, and the faeries vanished from sight.

"Julia? Are you back here?" Thomas called. "It's time to go, babe."

*****

Anna had finally agreed to rest and was napping in her bedroom. With her time so near and her condition delicate, Emma stayed close if Cade had to be away. Now was the perfect time for her daily meditation.

With great care, Emma placed a purple satin cloth on the end table before her, smoothing every crease and wrinkle until it was perfect. Next she pulled two white candles from her prayer satchel and lit them.

Which crystals should I use today?

She carefully touched each of her sacred stones until she decided on amethyst, citrine, and clear quartz, placing them in a triangle on the purple cloth.

Closing her eyes, she centered her mind and quieted her thoughts, opening herself to the Goddess and her spirit guides.

"Blessed be, my daughter," the Goddess greeted her, in a soft voice.

"Blessed be Mother. How may I be of service?"

"Two of my sons are on the verge of meeting their mates. Richie Majors, Anna's friend and your own son Lucas."

Emma gasped, and then whispered wide-eyed. "Lucas?"

"There is a very special woman waiting for him in Texas. My daughter, Krystal, will be instrumental in bringing them together."

"Is there anything you need me to do to help that along?"

"You must make sure Krystal leaves with him when he moves to Texas. I have additional reasons for her move, but I will disclose them at a later date. Once they settle in Texas, I will speak with you again with detailed instructions to ensure Lucas meets Miss Kensie Brown."

"I'll talk to Isaac and make sure his sister–in–law Lucinda does not prevent her from leaving," Emma promised.

"As for Richie, I have already set into motion the situation that will bring his mate into his life. His human friends who attend college here in Louisiana will make sure they meet."

"This is very exciting! Two more of our men will finally meet their mates after waiting so long."

"I am very pleased and I thank you for the assistance you have given me with many of them."

"It is always my pleasure to be of service to my, Mother Goddess," Emma said as she lowered her head in supplication.

"Take care, my daughter, blessed be."

"Thank you, Mother. Blessed be."

Bursting with excitement, Emma wrung her hands. "Why does everyone have to be either sleeping or away when I get news like this?"

She was just going to have to find something to distract herself until Anna woke up.

Cookies!

She could make a batch or three of cookies.

*****

She was taking the last sheet of baked chocolate chip cookies from the oven when she heard Cade walk through the door.

Thank Goddess! Isaac? Where are you?

I'm at home. Why?

I have the most incredible news! I'll be right there.

Not more than five minutes later, Emma walked through her door and into Isaac's waiting arms. He held her tightly before claiming her lips in a heart–stopping kiss.

"Have I told you today that I adore you, and you are my world?"

"No," Emma panted as she caught her breath. "I don't believe you have."

"Well, you incredibly sexy woman, I do." Isaac claimed her lips again until they were both dizzy from lack of oxygen.

"Keep that up and I'll forget my news."

"I was having a thought myself," he growled, nuzzling her neck.

"What was that?" she asked tilting her head to give him better access.

"We're only four hundred or so years old. Let's have another baby."

Emma stiffened. "Are you on crack, or whatever they are doing these days? You cut me off cold turkey over one hundred fifty years ago, insisting on no more children. I was the one who wanted to keep trying for a girl."

"I know, mon amour, I was wrong." Isaac nibbled on her earlobe, something that always got her engine running. "Just think about it and we can talk again later."

Emma groaned and stepped from Mr. Sex on a Stick's arms. "Okay, stop that. You're distracting me, and I have news."

With love bursting from his heart, he brushed a loose strand of hair behind her ear. "What's your news, cher?"

"The Goddess came to me today and told me several things. I think you should get a scotch and sit with me in the great room."

Isaac hesitated with a frown creasing his brow. "It wasn't bad news was it?"

"No." She shook her head laughing. "It's wonderful news but you may need to make a plan to handle Lucinda."

"Good, you had me worried for a second."

With a scotch in hand, he got comfortable with his mate on the couch. "Snuggle up close and tell me what you know."

Emma told him every word that had been said and then sat quietly while he thought them through.

"If it comes down to it, I will simply talk privately with Charles and then force her hand with a royal decree that she allow Krystal to move to Texas with Lucas. It's not like she has an actual say in her adult children's lives, but she's bullied them so terribly that they're afraid to go against her."

THOMAS: Le Beau Series

Emma shook her head sadly. "I have seen it too many times, especially with the girls. And I'm concerned about her mental health."

Isaac stroked her gorgeous hair. "She hasn't been right since, Armand."

"I know, but it's been long enough and something is going to have to be done."

"I'll talk to Charles again, but it's so hard for him to deny his mate anything."

"I know, mon amour, I know."

*****

Thomas was taking his turn in the shower, so Julia grabbed one of his cotton dress shirts to cover her nakedness while she made dinner. The salad was tossed, and Cajun chicken was in the oven roasting along with baked potatoes. All she needed was to let the wine breathe.

She was washing her hands after handling the chicken when Thomas joined her. She turned to look over the shoulder he had laid his chin on and kissed him sweetly.

His heart began to hammer, and his body instantly yelled an enthusiastic "YES!" He had her lips, and he'd be a fool to not take advantage of the situation. And as far as he knew, no one had ever called him a fool; he planned to keep it that way. With one hand gently wound in her hair, he kissed her again. She tasted like paradise, and his white button down shirt on her freshly showered, naked body was more than he could resist.

One kiss turned into many, and he lost track. Not that he was counting. He wanted her—again. Even though, they had made love the second they were home not forty–five minutes ago.

When he finally stopped long enough to lift his head, her eyes were glowing with her need of him. She smiled, her little shy 'I want you' smile that made his stomach do a flip.

"As much as it pains me to say it, give me a minute to clean up before someone gets salmonella. Then, you can carry me off like a caveman."

"Caveman?" he chuckled. "I was thinking the kitchen table looked the perfect height for what I have in mind for you. Every room and surface in this house needs to be christened."

"Christened? Is that what they're calling it these days?"

"Mmm, most definitely," he murmured, as he made another assault on her neck. "You've got two minutes before I strip you bare."

The pins in her hair fascinated him. How could a couple of straight wooden sticks hold all of her hair together? With a final kiss and nuzzle to her neck, he pulled each free, one by one, watching her hair flow freely down her back in a sensual wave. Damn, she was sexy, a mixture of dangerous and delicate.

He raked his fingers through the long silk several times before sliding his hands around to the buttons on her shirt. With each button, his knuckles brushed warm, bare skin, exposing the soft swell of her breasts. He was completely captivated by this little woman.

Finally, she set the dishrag aside so he could turn her in his arms. His gaze locked with hers. She wanted him as badly as he wanted her, he could see it in the way she consumed him with her glowing eyes.

THOMAS: Le Beau Series

"I need to taste you," he admitted hoarsely.

Thomas brushed the shirt from her shoulders and let it drop to the floor. Before this incredible woman entered his life, he'd been happy. At least he thought he had. He hadn't believed he would ever want a wife and family. Hell. He hadn't realized he was lonely. He'd set himself on a path of protecting those who needed him and service, first by attending the academy then being a private investigator and now head of security. Before Julia, that path had been enough. And then she'd calmly walked into his life and changed it forever.

Her warm, sure hands skimmed up his belly to his chest. Before she could wrap them around his neck, he caught them and pressed a kiss to the center of each palm. The look of need in her eyes sent another punch of desire low and sharp to his groin, stealing his breath. No woman had ever fueled such an urgent lust in him.

"You're killing me, woman," he groaned, gathering her closer, so her body molded against his. "I've never needed a woman like I need you."

His hands fisted in her hair, and as he tilted his head, his mouth took possession of hers to catch the soft, sexy sigh she always made right before he kissed her. God, he loved that little sound. His cock strained against his jeans and pressed against her belly as her hands snaked around his neck for support. Pumping his hips, he thrust rhythmically, he couldn't help it. Her tongue danced with his, fingers massaging the back of his neck while her body trembled with her own need.

He wanted her, right here, right now. Walking her backward to the kitchen table, he lifted her to sit on top. With one hand, he unbuttoned his jeans and tugged to get them the hell off. While he cupped the back of her head with the other, ravishing her mouth.

"I need you right now, Tommy, fast and hard," Julia demanded. "No soft kisses and petting, just fast, raw, sex."

Thomas groaned; her words were gasoline thrown on an already raging fire. She wanted fast and hard; she would get it.

Grabbing both of her hips, he pulled her forward as he thrust to the hilt. Julia moaned into his mouth as she continued to explore every nook and cranny. Gripping her ass he pounded into her as she clutched his shoulders and let her head drop back.

Moans and rumbles filled the room as they crested the summit together, Julia shouting his name as he shouted hers.

Ragged panting broke the silence as the scent of their lovemaking swirled in the air. Leaning his forehead against hers; they caught their breaths, crisp wintery snow and rich dark spices mingled and intertwined.

Once he was able to breathe fairly normally and stand on his noodlefied legs, he pulled his jeans over his hips and handed her the shirt from the floor. They were both exhausted and would have another busy day tomorrow. The rest of the evening's agenda was a quick dinner and sleep. Lots and lots of sleep.

*****

Dawn was sneaking in through the seams of the shade like a seasoned cat burglar. He was exhausted; last night's dreams had been bad, really bad. One dream after another of Julia disappearing or just out of reach, he was never able to reach quite far enough to pull her back to him.

But the last one, the one that woke him up in a cold sweat, was the worst. He had dreamt that none of the past days with her were real, and she didn't even know who he was.

Trembling, he kept his eyes closed, terrified if he opened them, the nightmare would be real. Tentatively he stretched his arm across the bed, feeling for a warm, soft body.

EMPTY!

His heart stopped beating.

No God, no. It can't be real!

When his head began to swim, he was forced to take a breath. He inhaled a lung full of her wintery scent.

Thank God! He sighed and opened his eyes.

You okay in there? Do you need me?

I'm perfect now. Why aren't you in my bed where you belong?

Goofball. I'm fixing your coffee.

You're too good for me.

Realizing what he said, he quickly added.

Ignore the man behind the curtain. Don't listen to him.

Her soft laughter tinkled like tiny bells in his mind. *I think you watched The Wizard of Oz too many times as a child.*

He grabbed the pillow beside him and inhaled Julia's scent until he was drunk with it. Throwing off the covers, he stretched his stress–stiffened muscles before padding barefoot to join her.

She was setting two mugs of fresh coffee on the table when he stepped through the door. The aroma blending with her scent was utter perfection, he couldn't think of a better aroma to start every day for the rest of his life. He knew he was grinning like an idiot, but he didn't care.

"You're so beautiful in the morning."

"Thank you. I think you're rather handsome, too. I better drink this while I dress. We ladies are going back to the bar to give it a good cleaning."

"I better get dressed too. I'm going with the men swamper hunting."

Thomas had grabbed a fresh pair of jeans from his drawer and now leaned on his dresser sipping his coffee and watching his woman intently.

His robe slipped from her shoulders, revealing the intricate tattoo on her back of some beautiful bird he couldn't name. The long tail feathers curled around her hip and back in, under the curve of her left buttock. He wanted to trail his tongue along that tail and see where it ended.

"Tell me about your tattoo," he said, tracing a finger along the realistic feathers.

"A few years ago, when I first decided to fight back against my mother's controlling ways, I had this tattoo done. It's both a 'fuck you' to her and a symbol for myself. It reminds me that I can rise up like the phoenix from the ashes and be a completely new woman. When I'm feeling depressed, I look at it with a mirror and remind myself all I need is the willpower, and I can do anything. Even defy her. Plus, wearing a revealing shirt to show it off around her friends is an added bonus."

"Please let me be there the next time you do that," he begged like a little boy.

THOMAS: Le Beau Series

"It's a date," she grinned and kissed him. "Now, let me get dressed."

She stepped away from him to pick out a t-shirt and jeans. She was cleaning today, so nothing fancy.

When she bent to step into her lace panties, he nearly spit his coffee across the room. She shimmied the scrap up her legs, the elastic molding her ass like a lover while a single lacy string disappeared from sight between her rounded cheeks.

"Dammit, Julia. I'm going to have a raging hard–on all day, thanks to you, and you know I can't shift well yet," he accused.

She glanced slyly over her shoulder, batting her long lashes. "Perfect. I want you imagining me naked all day while you're out doing manly stuff. That way, you'll be looking forward to seeing me tonight instead of thinking about any old girlfriends."

"I don't have old girlfriends, and Stefan is going to have a field day with this," he whined, indicating his pelvis.

"I'm sure you'll live."

Thomas dropped his head back, praying for strength. Blood pulsed in his groin as the memory of their encounter in the kitchen played in his mind like a movie. He struggled to swallow on a dry throat. Well, hell if you can't beat 'em, join 'em.

Stepping up behind her, he nuzzled her inviting neck before kissing his way to her earlobe. His palms skimmed down her arms and up to cup the weight of her breasts. Stroking his thumbs back and forth across her hardened nipples. Julia moaned, her soft body leaning against him, rubbing like a cat in heat.

V.A. Dold

I am imagining you at my feet, with your luscious lips stretched around my cock.

Really? Her arm came up around his neck to draw him to her lips. She drew his tongue into her mouth, sucking it like it was his dick.

All you had to do was ask.

Julia stepped from his arms and turned. Without breaking eye contact, she dropped to her knees and stripped his jeans to his ankles. His breath left his lungs in a rush as her warm wet mouth engulfed him. His eyes fluttered shut as she cupped his balls, rolling and squeezing gently as she bobbed up and down his length.

She took her time, her tongue circling the sensitive velvet head, lapping up the pearly drops seeping out. Thomas steadied his rubbery legs with a hand on her shoulder. Lord in heaven, her mouth was hot and wet, and–his eyes rolled back in his head– so damn tight.

Her tongue danced around the head of his cock like nothing he had ever experienced before. A fire raged in his groin, roaring for release.

"Baby, I'm going to cum."

He tried to pull her to her feet, but she only sucked harder insisting on finishing him. His balls pulled up tight readying for his release before he exploded into her.

Thomas's knees threatened to give out. He stood quivering, waiting for his brain to function again. Before he could jump-start the section of his brain that controlled speech, she stood and finished dressing with a knowing smile playing on her lips.

With still unsteady hands, he pulled his jeans over his hips again and fastened the button.

When he was finally able to form words, all he could say was, "Wow!"

"I'm glad you liked it. Plan on round two later," she said and licked her lips suggestively while staring at his cock.

"Dang it, woman, stop doing that!"

Chapter 16

The roar of outboard motors was loud in the still morning air as a parade of boats sped toward The Backwater bar. The women were armed with brooms, buckets, and mops while the men carried no weapons at all. Once they shifted to wolf form, they were the weapons. And besides, they would have no way to carry one except in their jaws.

Thomas offered his hand to Julia and helped her from their boat. Secretly, he prayed the electric tingle he got each time he touched her would never fade away.

One by one, each man who was mated helped his woman from the boat and held her close for a sweet goodbye.

Julia pressed closer to Thomas breathing warm air across his neck and whispered, "Don't forget, I have plans for you tonight." She gave his ear a long slow lick, smiling to herself as she felt him grow hard against her hip.

THOMAS: Le Beau Series

"You're an evil woman," Thomas growled, bunching a fist full of hair in his right hand and dragging her lips to his.

"I try," she breathed between kisses.

Lucas walked past and waved for them to join the group gathering on the yard behind the bar.

Thomas let Julia precede him and promptly gave her a swat on the butt for her naughty behavior.

She threw her head back and laughed. Goddess she loved teasing this man.

As the men talked quietly in smaller groups, Julia moved to the edge of the trees. One of the faeries was waving her arms to get her attention.

"Good morning, Princess Julia," the faeries said and curtsied. "Are the men going after the bad shifters today?"

"Yes, they are."

The little faerie stood a little taller, pride radiating from her tiny body. "We kept watch on your establishment all night. No one has come near it."

"Thank you, Petunia. I appreciate the care and concern you have shown to both me and Tommy."

Petunia blushed and whispered, "Prince Tommy is so handsome." The little bit of a faerie dragged out the word 'so' like a giddy teenager with a crush.

*****

Lucas looked over the crowd of volunteers and mentally chose teams. Then he considered the women, should he leave protection behind at The Backwater or not?

221

"Before I put you into teams, I'm wondering, does anyone feel we should leave a protection detail behind for the women?"

All the mated men immediately voiced their opinion, not wanting their mates alone at the bar, but the women felt differently.

El raised her voice first. "I think as shifters ourselves, we're able to handle anything that arises. Between myself, Rose, Emma, Julia, and Krystal, we can keep Anna safe and out of trouble."

Nods and murmurs of agreement were heard from all the women.

Isaac turned to Emma. "I don't like it, but it's your call."

Emma gave the women a good, hard look. "I think we will be fine. Besides in about six hours Jack and Michael will be here."

Cade squeezed Anna's hand. "I will abide by your decision; please make sure it's a safe one."

"I agree with El, we're more than capable of taking care of ourselves for a few hours."

It was plain as day which men were mated with women staying behind by the scowls on their faces. But the king and queen along with their future queen had made a decision, and they had to live by it.

"All right, I'm going to split you into three teams. Isaac, Marcus, Charles, Logan, and myself are team one. Cade, Simon, John, and Etienne, you are team two. Thomas, Stefan, Quin, Rémi, and René, you are team three."

The women kissed their mates goodbye while the men reassembled with their teammates to await further instructions.

THOMAS: Le Beau Series

"We will spread out from the water's edge near the bar and work our way into the forest. Keep in mind, these backward-thinking swampers are experts at hiding. Isaac, would you like to tell everyone about your meeting with Queen Lilli?"

Isaac stepped to the front of the group next to Lucas. "Lilli has asked to be present at the swampers' executions. She has every right to locate and kill these animals herself, and I was more than happy to agree with her request. As such, once the swampers are apprehended, I will call Lilli to join us before I mete out the justice they deserve."

All of the men agreed, Lilli was being more than fair and should be in attendance.

"Go to your positions and shift, Isaac will signal for us to begin."

Thomas led his group to the far right of the line; Isaac was center, and Cade was on the left.

In the blink of an eye, Thomas found himself surrounded by wolves as he attempted to shift for a second time. Stefan chuffed at his naked, very erect condition, earning a growl from Thomas and a smack on the head from Isaac's paw. Three times the charm and Thomas was ready to kick swamper ass.

Wolves of every color slipped into the trees sniffing, searching for a trail to follow.

*****

Julia ushered the women into The Backwater. The reaction of gaping mouths and wide eyes was universal as the women saw the empty space for the first time.

"Damn, they really did a number on the place," El grumbled.

"You should have seen it yesterday," Julia sighed as she held back tears.

Emma put an arm around her shoulders. "We'll have it better than new in a jiffy."

"I know," she shrugged. "The one bonus is Logan can decorate any way he wants now."

"Why is he decorating your bar?" Rose asked.

"I'm selling out to him and living with Tommy at the plantation. It's too far to travel by boat each day to continue operating it myself."

Squeals of excitement echoed in the empty space as the women welcomed Julia and started cleaning. Well, all except Anna. Seated on the only chair, that was still in one piece, she acted as lookout in case of trouble.

Sweat poured off Julia as she scrubbed the back bar prep area. Every surface needed to be wiped and sanitized before it could be restocked with bottles and glassware.

Standing straight to stretch her back, Julia arched to relief the ache. She took this little stretch break to check on the others. Everyone worked diligently, talking little. The chatter had died off two hours ago.

As she reached for her spray bottle, Anna shouted an alarm.

"What are you doing here?" she yelled at whoever was docking a boat. "You can't be here!"

Emma stopped sweeping. "Who's out there, cher?" she called.

Anna was shaking like a leaf. "Tim," she squeaked before she disappeared from their view.

THOMAS: Le Beau Series

*****

The men had been systematically searching in a grid pattern for the past four hours when Logan caught a trace of lingering trail. All fourteen men took turns learning the scent and searching for the path the swampers had taken. As Thomas stepped forward to give it a sniff, Petunia and Tulip hovered before him, waving their arms to get his attention.

"We know where they are," Tulip whispered.

Thomas couldn't speak to them in wolf form, so he shifted back to human. "Where?" he whispered back.

Petunia waved for him to follow her into thick cover hiding a game trail. He stayed in human form while the others followed as wolves. They worked their way through alternating heavy cover and soggy ground for over a mile until she stopped at the base of a large cypress.

"Why are we stopping?" Thomas wondered.

"They are here," Petunia whispered, pointing at the tree.

Thomas looked left and right, then leaned closer to the tiny faerie. "Where?"

"Here," Tulip pointed as she landed on the huge trunk.

When Thomas continued to look confused, Petunia landed next to Tulip with her hands on her hips. "Can't you see the door?"

That's when he noticed a thread-thin crack in the trunk that, when followed, was shaped like an arch.

"Do you know how to open it?" he asked the faeries.

Petunia giggled while Tulip rolled her eyes. "Of course."

She tapped a dark patch on the trunk, and the arch fell open.

"Damn," Thomas breathed. "We would have never found that."

The space would never accommodate a human, so he shifted back to wolf while the others began to file through the hole and into a tunnel.

Etienne crossed his arms and glanced at Isaac. "Call me when you either find the little bastards or reach the other end and I will join you."

Isaac's wolf nodded and slipped through the opening behind the last wolf.

The tunnel ran just under the surface for a city block or so before it exited another cypress. Isaac lifted his nose to the breeze to locate Etienne's direction, and then sent Rémi to fetch the vampire. The others spread out in teams again to locate the swampers trail. By the time Etienne rejoined the search, a fresh scent had been discovered. And based on the strength of the scent trail, the swampers had just passed this way.

The wolves silently crept along a well–established game trail until voices broke the serene atmosphere.

"I would have paid good money to see the look on that bitch's face when she saw her house," one man bragged.

"Yeah. Me, too. Dumb skank should have accepted what I had to offer. Having the Benevolent Sovereign order the strike right after she attacked us was perfect timing. Not that I wouldn't have retaliated, but this way it was sanctioned," Blade agreed.

Lucas signaled for the teams to fan out for the attack; they needed to take them alive if possible for Queen Lilli.

THOMAS: Le Beau Series

The five swampers sat around what looked like a makeshift camp, unaware danger lurked in every direction.

Isaac used his ability to communicate with all of his subjects to issue the command to attack.

Surprised shouts and squeals were heard as thirteen wolves, and one very pissed off vampire leapt into the camp. Immediately the swampers shifted, ready to fight to the death.

Isaac allowed the shift, more for the men to have a chance to avenge the attack on their family than anything else. He would let them fight it out for a bit before he forced the swampers to human form.

One swamper was spinning circles as Lucas attacked its head and Marcus its flank. Lucas slashed the swamper's muzzle with his razor sharp fangs, sending a stream of blood down its chest and filling the air with its coppery scent. Before the wolf could recover, Marcus leapt on its back, latching onto its neck with his powerful jaws.

The rest of Team One – Isaac, Charles, and Logan had another mangy wolf on defense. Isaac crouched ready to pounce, and Charles and Logan took turns snapping at its hind legs. The second the swamper lifted its jaw high enough, Isaac latched onto its neck, immobilizing the beast.

Team Two looked almost bored with their target. Four on one didn't offer much sport. While Etienne shot stinging energy at the wolf's ass every chance he got, Cade, Simon, and John took a bit of fur here and there with each lunging attack. Taking the wolf down would end the fight, and they weren't ready for that to happen.

Quin, Rémi, and René kept their swamper busy and increasingly bloody while Thomas and Stefan took on Blade.

Blade lunged for Thomas's left forepaw, snapping air when Thomas jumped out of reach at the last second. While Blade concentrated on Thomas, Stefan latched onto his right hind leg with a grip so tight the sound of bones cracking resounded in the air. When Blade reached around to rip at Stefan, Thomas clamped his jaws down on Blade's neck. Blade tried to struggle free, but quickly learned that that, only caused the wolf at his neck to rip his flesh further. Growling and snarling, Blade stilled, waiting for Thomas to either finish him off or make a mistake.

All the swampers were subdued except Cade's group. They were still toying with theirs.

Charles, take charge of this idiot. I'm going to force them to shift so be ready, Isaac commanded. Then he warned the rest of the crew that the swampers were being forced to human form.

Lucas shifted, ready to grab their swamper as Marcus released the wolf in order to shift himself. The instant Marcus let go, and the shifter became human, the swamper tried to make a run for it. Lucas swept the swamper's legs out from under him as Marcus leapt on his back and followed him to the ground landing with an "ummph" as the air was forced from his lungs.

Isaac waited for Charles and Logan to shift, before he released their swamper and forced the shift on the mangy wolf. An instant later, Isaac, too, stood in human form as Charles and Logan held the swamper securely between them.

THOMAS: Le Beau Series

Etienne was frustrated; he wanted a fight, and this was not satisfying his need to avenge the attack on his friends. The instant the wolves stepped away to shift, he flicked a finger toward the swamper, shooting a strong bolt of energy at the man's chest as he took human form and knocking him out cold.

Quin waited for his brothers to shift before releasing their target and taking human form. Rémi and René grabbed the swamper before he could make a dash for freedom, and stood waiting for Isaac's next command.

The only wolves remaining were Thomas, Stefan, and Blade. Stefan shifted first and then crouched in a ready stance to allow Thomas to release Blade's neck. The instant Blade felt Thomas's jaws loosen he tried to attack but found himself flattened to the ground unable to move.

Thomas stood and shifted, managing to redress himself on his second try, and stood breathing heavily, glaring at Blade.

"Let me up, you fucking coward. Are you afraid to fight me?" Blade demanded, as he struggled against Etienne's magic, which held him glued to the ground.

"I would like nothing more than to grant your wish. Alas, Queen Lilli wants to be present for your execution, so I must wait."

Isaac spotted Petunia hiding in a bush and waved her over. Hardly able to fly from her quivering, she hovered unsteadily before the shifter king.

"Please, call Queen Lilli to us."

Petunia curtsied and sped away.

Isaac motioned for Thomas and Stefan to pick their trash up off the ground. "Blaaaade," he growled, his tone intentionally lethal as he dragged out Blade's name.

"You have one chance and only one chance. Who is this Benevolent Sovereign?"

Blade spat blood at Isaac's feet. "As if I would tell you, the temporary king who is about to fall."

Isaac raised an eyebrow at Etienne, knowing the vampire was dying for some action. A huge grin spread across Etienne's face, and he happily shot a bolt of energy at Blade's forehead and watched him crumble in the hands of Thomas and Stefan.

"He should be out cold for at least fifteen minutes. I would be happy to incapacitate the others as well," Etienne offered with a hopeful grin.

Isaac looked over the still conscious but bloody swampers. "Would you prefer to await your death with Blade or keep your wits about you?"

All three swampers were quick to say they would cooperate.

"Thank you, Etienne, but for now I won't require your services."

Isaac threw back his head and laughed as Etienne pouted, actually pouted!

A shower of sparkles preceded Queen Lilli's appearance. Like an angry bee, she shot from one swamper to the next, causing them to scream in agony as she touched them.

Finally, she hovered before King Isaac, smoothing her gown. "Sorry about that–I lost my temper. Shall we begin?"

Isaac looked at Etienne and waved his hand at the two shifters out cold. "Do you have any magic in your bag of tricks to bring those two around?"

THOMAS: Le Beau Series

Without turning to look at the swampers in question, Etienne flicked a finger over his shoulder and a second bolt of energy shocked them awake.

Isaac grinned at his longtime friend. "Thank you."

Clearing his throat, he addressed the prisoners. "You are guilty of attacking a member of the royal family and are sentenced to die. Any one of you who tells me the identity of the Benevolent Sovereign will receive a quick and painless death. All others will be handed over to Queen Lilli to receive what I have witnessed to be a long and agonizing death. This sentence is handed down as punishment for the death of Daffi, one of her royal subjects."

"No one speaks," Blade yelled as he glared at Isaac.

The king sighed. "So be it." He turned his attention to the queen and said, "Lilli, again I offer you condolences for your loss. The only thing I can give you to ease your pain is the guilty parties to do with as you please."

"Thank you, Isaac. If you ever need my assistance, all you need do is get word to me." She gave him a regal nod, snapped her fingers and disappeared along with the swampers.

Suddenly, Thomas spun to face the direction of The Backwater, shifted and tore off like a bat out of hell.

*****

Everyone was momentarily stunned. Tim wasn't supposed to be able to enter the state. Etienne had cursed him so his manly bits and pieces would fall off if he ever tried. How was this possible?

Julia stared at the now empty doorway. This wasn't a joke and it looked like a fight was headed their way.

She leapt the bar and rushed the door; no one was going to threaten a pregnant woman, especially her mother–in–law. Not on her watch.

The slap and clank of mops and brooms hitting the floor echoed around the large, empty, space.

Emma, Rose, Krystal, and El watch Julia clear the door frame ready to do battle, but, instead of a fist hitting flesh, they heard a cry of pain followed by silence.

"Anna! Julia!" Emma cried. This couldn't be happening. All three women skidded to a halt as they crossed into the fading light of day. Julia lay unconscious at a hideous man's feet, and Anna whimpered in fear as she was held as a shield in front of him.

"Goddess! Does he have leprosy or something?" Rose whispered to El.

"No," Emma answered, anger lacing her tone. "Etienne cursed him for abusing Anna, and what you see is the punishment for disobeying his orders. I imagine he is in a world of hurt as his private parts mummify and begin to fall off."

The women gasped at Emma's description of his condition. But there was no time to hesitate, Anna was in danger and the stress of the situation could put her into labor.

"Get back!" Tim demanded, and he pressed the gun he held harder into Anna's temple.

"What is it you want, Mr. James," Emma asked in a steady voice.

"I have what I want," he spat as he forced Anna to move closer to the pier.

Suddenly a howl rose deep in the forest, long and mournful and moving toward them. Help was coming, and, from the sound of it, it was coming fast.

THOMAS: Le Beau Series

"Move it, bitch," Tim snarled, pushing Anna towards his boat.

He hadn't gone three steps when a monstrous, slathering wolf crashed from the forest. Growling menacingly, it paced around him as if looking for an opportunity to attack.

Tim was about to be seriously disappointed; there was no way he was moving another step with Thomas's mother. And the site of Julia lying prone on the ground was the seal on his death warrant. Tim James would not see another day, today he would breathe his last breath on this earth.

This was about to get bloody, and Thomas was going to be the one bringing the pain. There was one small problem; first he needed his mother safe and Tim away from the women. He watched, uncaring as his father reposition the gun and pointed it at him. He didn't care; he'd take a bullet if it gave the women the chance to get his mother away from his psychotic father.

Anna watched as her son, in wolf form, faced off with his father. She had to do something. She considered the consequences of head–butting Tim with a gun to her head. Would the gun go off, leaving Cade without his mate to follow her into death? She couldn't have that, nor could she lose the baby she carried, and she certainly wouldn't lose her son. She looked at Emma and her sisters–in–law, all who stood frozen and snarling, too afraid to move or shift for fear he would shoot her.

Tears of frustration welled in her eyes. She wasn't one to allow another person to make her this helpless, but she also couldn't put her baby in jeopardy. The wolf in her wanted to tear the idiot to shreds, regardless of the consequences. But her human side knew that wasn't an option–it wasn't worth the risk. No, she would have to watch for an opening before she could make her move.

Before she could formulate a plan, Tim removed the pressure of the gun barrel from her temple and pointed it at Thomas.

"No!" she cried, as a silenced gunshot popped next to her ear. She watched as Thomas staggered, and the sight of blood soaking his shoulder was more than she could take. As if on autopilot, her fury and instincts took over. She slammed her head back into his face. A loud crunch resounded behind her head, telling her she had hit her mark. Tim screamed in pain, releasing her to grasp his bloody, crushed nose with both hands.

Immediately, Emma jumped at the chance to rescue Anna, pulling and her away from Tim and shoving her behind her body. In the same instant, Rose and El grabbed Julia and drug her closer to the bar door and behind them while Krystal snatched the gun from the ground where Tim dropped it.

The sudden pain from the bullet graze on his shoulder triggered Thomas to shift back to human. He ignored the burning ache radiating from the gunshot wound; his mother and Julia were both safely away. Now he could get down to business.

Tim watched with an expression of horror on his face as the rabid wolf became his son. "What the hell are you?"

"Your worst nightmare," Thomas replied in an ominously quiet tone. "You should've stayed in Vegas. Coming here was your first mistake, touching my mate, and my mother was your last."

Tim's head snapped to the right as Thomas smashed his fist into his jaw. Using his shifter speed, Thomas

THOMAS: Le Beau Series

grabbed the front of Tim's shirt and held him upright. He wasn't done with this asswipe, and there was no way he was letting him go down that easy. Several more punches to the face and countless jabs to his midsection and Tim resembled a hanging beef carcass in a butcher shop. Blood cover both men and the ground around them. Between the sores and boils a la Etienne, a smashed nose compliments of Anna, and Thomas's beating, his face was ground beef. The only injuries Thomas sustained, however, were bloodied knuckles and the bullet graze to his shoulder.

Thomas was done with this piece of shit. Julia still lay unmoving, and he needed to get to her. Jerking Tim's unconscious body close, he wrapped his hands around his head and chin ready to snap his neck like a twig.

"Thomas, leave him to me," Etienne said as he stepped from the forest. While Thomas had been using Tim as a punching bag, the search party had arrived.

Thomas didn't acknowledge Etienne, so he spoke again. "I will hold him while you take care of your mate. See to her health, he isn't going anywhere."

He hesitated for a moment. He really wanted to end this bastard's existence, but the need to care for Julia was stronger.

"He's mine; no one else touches him."

Roughly, he shoved Tim away from him and toward Etienne, and rushed to Julia's side. He wrapped his arms around her, desperate to hear her breath and her heartbeat. She was alive, but why wouldn't she open her eyes?

"Julia, baby, talk to me," the agonized plea tore from his throat as he pulled her into his arms. She was so still–too still.

A pool of blood had formed under her head, and his fingers desperately felt for the wound so he could put pressure on it to stop the bleeding.

FUCK!

There wasn't just a head wound; she had been shot in the back as well.

He couldn't breathe, and tears blurred his vision. The only thing that held him together was the sound of her steady heartbeat.

"Mom, Grandma, help me!" he cried as he rocked her prone body.

"Don't you dare die, Julia. Fight dammit! I need you to come back to me," he begged as he laid Julia on her stomach to check the severity of the wound.

Thomas carefully searched every inch of his mate, but there was no exit wound to be found. The bullet was still inside Julia. There was no way they could move her by boat to reach an emergency room in her condition. Any medical attention would have to happen right here, right now, in these unsterile conditions.

Isaac put a gentle hand on Thomas's shoulder. "Son, I know it's difficult, but you need to let the women take care of her now. Stand up and take a step back. We'll stay close in case the women need us."

Reluctantly, Thomas kissed Julia's cheek and did as he was told. His wolf fought to stay with its fallen mate, and Thomas's heart agreed, but in his mind he knew these women were her only hope.

Cade helped Anna kneel while Emma dropped to her knees on the other side of Julia. Quickly, the women assessed the situation.

"We need to get the bullet out first. Ladies, please place your hands on my back and shoulders and imagine energy flowing through you and into me. Some of you men, do the same for Anna," Emma directed.

In a heartbeat, the yard was a blur of dashing shifters as men and women rushed to lend aid. Closing their eyes, Anna and Emma sent a stream of healing energy through Julia, focusing on forcing the bullet to exit, following the path it had forged.

Thomas thought he was going to lose his mind. The healers were taking too long. In reality, the women had only been working on Julia for a matter of minutes, but to him it was a lifetime. He watched as a heavy stream of blood was pushed from the wound followed by the spent bullet. In relief, he exhaled a breath he hadn't realized he was holding. *That's done. Now, get down to healing, dammit!*

His mother and grandmother we're putting everything that they had into healing his mate. Even with the extra energy flowing to them, it didn't seem to be enough. The bullet was out, the wound closed, and the laceration to her head healed, *why wasn't she waking up?*

"What's wrong?" he asked in a terrified voice. "Fix her, please."

Pale and swaying with weariness, Emma looked up at her grandson. "We've done all we can. She's lost too much blood. I'm sorry, cher, all we can do is wait and hope to get her to a hospital on time."

"No!" he wailed, fighting against the hold Isaac had on him.

"No!" he wailed, fighting against the hold Isaac had on him.

No one had noticed Petunia and Tulip wringing their hands in distress. Tulip turned to Petunia with tears streaming down her face. "Bring her, we need her now."

Petunia vanished with a tiny pop and reappeared moments later with Lilli.

Lilli gasped when she saw Julia pale and almost lifeless lying on the ground. She was a bright, colorful streak through the air as she rushed to Julia's aid.

"Please. Allow me to help."

"Can you save her?" Thomas asked, desperate for Lilli to say yes.

"I can. I just need a moment of silence."

The crowd became deathly still, with only the sound of breathing heard as everyone watched and prayed.

Thomas struggled with his frantic need to hold his mate, fear for her pushing him to his limit. Just when he couldn't take another second, Julia's eyes fluttered open, and she drew a deep breath.

Isaac released Thomas and stepped back allowing him to rush to his mate and assure himself she was, indeed, healed.

Thomas snatched her into his arms. "Thank Goddess. Don't ever put me through that again! Are you okay, baby, does it hurt anywhere?"

Thomas was holding her so tightly she couldn't breathe. Struggling, she pushed against his chest so she could draw a breath.

"You're crushing me, Thomas."

"Oh shit, I'm so sorry. I thought I'd lost you, I didn't mean to squeeze so hard."

Julia blinked at him as confusion set in. "What happened anyway? Anna said Tim was here and disappeared from sight. But that's the last thing I remember."

"Yeah. The bastard is over there. He shot you and hit you over the head with something. You almost died. We have my Mom, Grandmother, and Queen Lilli to thank for your life."

He helped her to her feet and reassured himself that she was in fact healed before he turned toward Etienne and his father.

"Charles, would you please take care of Julia for me for a minute."

Thomas waited for Charles to step forward and wrap an arm around his daughter before he turned toward Etienne.

Frowning in confusion, she watched as Thomas stalked menacingly up to the bloody man held by the vampire king.

"Bitch was supposed to die!" Tim hissed, bloody bubbles leaking from the corner of his mouth.

"If you wouldn't mind, I would appreciate it if you held him upright by his arms for me," Thomas said to Etienne in a calm voice that belied the red haze of fury churning within.

Etienne gave him a single nod. The one thing he couldn't abide was seeing a woman disrespected or bullied, and if the offender abused the woman physically or emotionally, he died, no questions – no second chances. Tim would die this day, either by Thomas's hand or his own. Anyone cowardly enough to victimize a weaker individual, especially a woman or child, deserved the most painful death conceivable. And if punishment was delivered by him – all the better. But this was Thomas's kill, and he would respect that.

Then Thomas looked John directly in the eye and said. "This ends here. You okay with that?"

John nodded, swallowing an obvious lump in his throat. There was no redemption for their father, not after everything he'd done to them, especially to Thomas. He just hated the idea his brother would live with the guilt of their father's death for the rest of his life. But he also knew Thomas needed to be the one to put him down. He needed the finality and closure that watching someone else executing Tim wouldn't bring.

Ignoring the crowd around him, Thomas turned his attention back to his father.

"Ready to die, old man?"

Tim made a snide face and laughed. "You're not going to kill me."

Without another word, not a blink, not a goodbye, Thomas shifted his right hand to a wolf paw with lethal, sharp claws and slashed Tim. Slicing him from stem to stern. Blood gurgled from his mouth as his organs and intestines bulge through gaping, bloody gashes.

When his father's chest rose in yet another breath, Thomas pulled his right paw back and sliced across Tim's jugular. This piece of shit would never come after his family, ever again.

Thomas turned toward Julia; the mixture of relief and concern marring his handsome face stole her breath.

Chapter 17

Two weeks later

Lucas closed and locked the large doors on the back of the moving van. Much of their furniture and household items were being professionally moved, but some things Lucas didn't trust to the movers, those he wanted to handle himself.

The entire family had gathered to say goodbye to Lucas and Krystal, and now stood around the van and assorted cars caravanning to the new ranch in the hill country of Texas. Well, all except Krystal's mother, Lucinda, who refused to come. She was dead set against Krystal moving and had tried to force her to stay. In the end, Isaac had stepped in and overruled Lucinda, earning him an enemy in the family. Thankfully, Charles didn't see things the way his wife did and had joined the group to kiss his baby girl goodbye and wish her well.

One by one, parents and siblings hugged them, acting like they were moving to the other side of the world instead of eight hours away. Finally, Emma stepped forward – she had waited at the back of the crowd until all the farewells had been said.

"Lucas, you've always taken care of Krystal like she was your sister. No doubt you'll watch over her now. I packed you lunch and snacks for the road as well as drinks in the cooler. Please drive safely and call me when you get there."

"I will, Mama, don't worry. And I'll keep Thomas and Julia out of trouble, too," he indicated the couple behind him with his thumb over his shoulder, and then stage whispered. "You know how trouble tends to find them."

Thomas chuckled as he whacked Lucas's Stetson off his head. "I think I'll be the one keeping you out of trouble with the local ranchers when you break their daughters' hearts."

After the attack at The Backwater, Thomas and Julia decided to take a vacation and help Lucas and Krystal move to the ranch and settle into their new home. A little change of scenery would do them both good and give them a chance to enjoy being newly mated without the day–to–day pressures of parents and Thomas's security responsibilities.

One by one, the van and cars drove down the long driveway and out of sight. Isaac tightened his arm around Emma as he glanced down and noticed a single tear rolling down her cheek. She always cried when her boys left on an adventure, but she never complained.

"Who's ready for a barbecue?" He'd figured out a long time ago that if he planned a family gathering the night one of the boys left, Emma recovered from the loss more quickly.

THOMAS: Le Beau Series

Happy shouts of people prepared for a party echoed around the yard.

"Meet us on the back deck at three p.m. for sweet tea and cocktails," Isaac shouted. Reaching for Emma, he walked hand and hand with the love of his life back to the house so she could collect herself in private.

*****

Krystal sat the last box of kitchen glassware on the granite countertop and stretched her back. That was the last of the breakables she had moved herself.

Now for food and household supplies; it had been a long drive to the ranch, but groceries weren't going to buy themselves.

"Julia, are you up to going to the store with me? Mother Hubbard's cupboards are bare, and I think it may take two carts to stock the kitchen."

"Sure. I noticed Emma hid steaks and potato salad in the bottom of the cooler for dinner, but I won't survive without coffee in the morning. Plus, I don't even want to think about things like using the bathroom and finding there's no toilet paper."

"Let's tell the guys where we're going and head out before it gets dark. Lucas would never let me hear the end of it if I got lost on these country back roads and he had to call him to come find us."

"I can hear him now," Julia said, rolling her eyes.

Lucas and Thomas waved as the women left, then continued unloading the truck. They wanted to come along, but someone needed to stay at the ranch. The movers were scheduled to arrive this afternoon, and they would need instructions on where to place the furniture.

V.A. Dold

Lucas had lucked out, not only did he manage to find a large, usable cattle ranch for sale, but the existing dude ranch on the next spread was also for sale. So, he bought both and had a website designed. Everyone had been shocked when reservations began to pour in. Now, they only had four short weeks to prepare the main house and guest cabins before people started arriving at the dude ranch. Not to mention hiring cowboys, buying horses, and stocking the ranch with a herd.

Julia's eyes grew wide as she read over the grocery list Krystal had written; it was large enough to fill a legal pad. "It's amazing how much stuff people normally have in their pantry and refrigerator that they take for granted. When you have to start from scratch, it's a bit mind-boggling."

"And that list is only what I need for the main house. Tomorrow we will start a list of items we need for the guest cabins. We don't even have beds or dressers in them."

Julia gaped open-mouthed at her sister. "It's a dang good thing we came along to help."

"You have no idea," Krystal laughed.

They each grabbed a shopping cart from the cart room as they entered the local grocery. If they worked the store row by row and kept moving, they would make it home in time to have cocktails with the guys and barbecue the steaks.

Krystal was studying the yogurt options when two women parked a cart close to her and started discussing cottage cheese choices.

She glanced at them, ready to introduce herself when she noticed the aura of the taller of the two. How interesting, the colors and pattern were identical to

Lucas's aura. As she examined the fluctuating colors more closely, the woman's spirit guide stepped forward.

"Kensie is your cousin, Lucas's, soul mate. Please help her."

Krystal gave the spirit guide a slight nod; careful no one saw her talking to an invisible entity. Few people knew her secret, not only could she see and read auras, but she could see everyone's spirit guides and speak to them.

Her breath caught in her throat. She could hardly believe it! Lucas's mate was standing not three feet from her.

Shaking off the shock, she cleared her throat. "Hello, my name is Krystal. I just moved to town. Do you live around here?"

The younger woman, the one with dark brown hair and large blue eyes, smiled brightly. "Hi! Yes, I do, and it's nice to meet you. I'm Jolene, but my friends call me Jojo, and this is my big sister, Kensie. I'm fairly new, too. I only moved here myself about six months ago. You're going to love it here. Everyone I've met is very friendly."

"It's wonderful to meet you both. So, you said you moved here, Jojo. Do you live somewhere else, Kensie?"

"Yes, I'm only visiting for a week, then I need to head back to Minnesota."

"Oh, that's too bad. I was going to invite you both to dinner once we get unpacked."

"Thank you, but I only came to make sure Jojo was doing okay. I have patients waiting for me back home so I can't stay."

"Yeah, Kensie is a famous doctor at the Mayo Clinic and has a waiting list about a mile long. I practically had to kidnap her to get her to take a few days off and come see me."

"If you would like to come to dinner, Jojo, I would love to have you over."

Jojo practically squealed. "I'd love to. Here's my number. Just call me when you're finished unpacking."

Krystal took her information and said goodbye before she moved to the next aisle. Her excitement at meeting Lucas's mate practically crackled in the air. She would have to come up with a plan to get Kensie to visit again so she could introduce her to Lucas.

Kensie was gorgeous, with her long red hair and large hazel eyes. Lucas had a thing for redheads, and she was going to knock him on his ass when he met her. Now, she just needed to figure out a way to get them together. How the heck was she going to accomplish that if the woman never took time off from her busy schedule?

Krystal tapped her pen on her chin as she puzzled it out. A call to Aunt Emma might be in order. She was the sneakiest person she knew, and might have an idea how she could get Kensie to come to visit again. Texas was going to be much more interesting than she expected.

The End

About the Author

V.A. Dold is the author of the **Le Beau Brothers** series, New Orleans wolf shifter novels. A graduate of Saint Cloud University, she majored in marketing with a minor in reading romance paperbacks.

Prior to becoming a full time writer, she was Publicist to the authors, owning ARC Author & Reader Conventions. Still is.

Her idea of absolute heaven is a day in the French Quarter with her computer, coffee mug and the brothers, of course.

A Minnesota native with her heart lost to Louisiana, she has a penchant for titillating tales featuring sexy men and strong women. When she's not writing, she's probably taking in a movie, reading, or traveling.

Her earliest reading memories are from grade school. She had a major fixation with horses, and the Black Stallion was a favorite. Then junior high came along and teenage hormones kicked in. It became all about the Harlequin Romances. She has been hooked on romances ever since.

Connect with V.A. Dold:

Visit V.A.'s Website http://www.vadold.com/
Like on Faceboook
https://www.facebook.com/pages/VA–
Dold/1404660546458551?ref=hl
Follow on twitter at https://twitter.com/
Goodreads https://www.goodreads.com/user/show/53
56266–v–a–dold

Read on for an excerpt from

V.A. Dold's

Next book:

RICHIE

Book 5
of the Le Beau Brothers

Prologue: The Plan

Emma Le Beau did a little happy dance. It was a rare moment in the home of the shifter King and Queen; the house was quiet. Before anyone could knock on her door, she snatched the perfect opportunity for her daily meditation.

With great care, she placed a purple, satin cloth on the altar she had consecrated to the Goddess Luperica centuries ago. The Goddess created the wolf shifters long ago when she blessed a village of humans with wolf souls. They became the first shifters. Since then she has only blessed a handful of humans that were not destined mates for a born shifter.

She carefully smoothed every crease and wrinkle until the altar cloth was perfect. Next she pulled two white candles from her prayer satchel and lit them.

V.A. Dold

Which crystals should I use today?

Gently, she touched each of her sacred stones until she decided on Amethyst, Citrine, and Clear Quartz. With the greatest reverence, Emma placed them in a triangle on her sacred purple cloth.

She closed her eyes, centered her mind, and quieted her thoughts. Opening herself to her spirit guides, and to the Goddess.

"Blessed be, my daughter," the Goddess greeted her in her soft, soothing voice.

"Blessed be, Mother. How may I be of service?"

"Two of my sons are on the verge of meeting their mates: Richie Majors, and your son, Lucas."

Emma gasped, and then whispered wide-eyed, "Both Richie and Lucas? Is there anything you would have me do to assist you with these matings?"

"My daughter Krystal, Lucas's cousin, will be instrumental. She must be allowed to move with him to Texas. But that we will discuss at a later date. I have already set into motion the situation that will bring Richie and his mate together. His human friends who attend college here in Louisiana will make sure they meet. He will be invited to attend a wedding. He must attend."

"If it pleases you, I could have Isaac talk with Richie's place of employment to guarantee he is given the days off he will need to attend."

"It does indeed please me," the Goddess said with a loving smile. "Also, if Richie hesitates in any way in regards to attending the wedding, he must be strongly encouraged to attend."

"Is there anything more I can do to be of service?" Emma asked.

THOMAS: Le Beau Series

"I am very pleased with everything you do. I am most pleased by the assistance you have provided; assuring these new humans are introduced to their destined mate and brought into the fold."

"It is always my pleasure to be of service to my mother Goddess," Emma said as she lowered her head in supplication.

"Take care, my most precious daughter. Blessed be."

"Take care, Mother. Blessed be."

Bursting with excitement, Emma wrung her hands. "Why does everyone have to be either sleeping or away when I get news like this?"

*****

By the time Isaac returned, Emma was on the verge of bursting. "Isaac! I have another name. Well, actually two names. Richie is going to meet his mate through friends. The Goddess requested that we ensure he gets the time off work to attend the wedding where he will meet her, and to also encourage him to go to that wedding if he gets wishy-washy."

"Who is the other?" Isaac asked, grinning at his mate's excitement.

"I was waiting for you to ask. Lucas! Can you believe it? And Krystal will be instrumental in bringing them together. Our job is to make sure she moves to Texas with him.

"We both know the only person who will try to stop her is her mother. I'll handle Lucinda. Now, whose wedding is Richie supposed to attend?"

"One of the girls he hangs out with from the college."

"Oh, I know that group of ladies. Richie talks about them all the time. He has even suggested that they be invited to a gathering, but without a shifter in their family, I can't take that chance."

"I agree, inviting them would be too risky."

"I'll stop by the Crescent City Brewhouse and chat with him about the wedding, you know, get a few details to work with."

Emma giggled like a schoolgirl. "I do love matchmaking our men."

"So do I," Isaac laughed, "As long as we don't get caught."

Isaac chuckled again and poured himself a Scotch. "This is very exciting! Lucas and Richie," Isaac shook his head. "That's just wonderful."

Humming happily to himself, he lounged with Emma in their great room as he sipped his scotch reminiscing. Isaac and his mate, Emma, had been successfully arranging for their sons to 'accidentally' meet their mates for over a year. So far, Cade, Simon, Stefan, and Thomas were all mated. In addition, they had received a bonus when Thomas's mate had turned out to be Julia, his brother Charles's daughter. And the frosting on this mating game cake was they now had a grandchild due any day. Life was pretty dang good.

He was very proud of the way he had gotten Emma, his exotically beautiful combination of Romanian gypsy and voodoo priestess, to petition the wolf-Goddess, Luperca to disclose the names of their sons' mates. Since the Goddess had revealed Anna as Cade's mate and where she would be on a specific day at a specific time, the names of additional mates had been steadily revealed.

All of their sons were following in his footsteps and

mating beautiful, curvaceous women. After two centuries, his Emma's exotic, sparkling dark eyes and compact, soft, killer curves still left him breathless. As a matter of fact, he was trying to talk her into giving him another child; maybe they would finally have a daughter?

Yes, I'm definitely going to have to work on that.

V.A. Dold

Enjoy the entire Le Beau Series
Book 1 CADE
Book 2 SIMON
Book 3 STEFAN
Book 4 THOMAS
Book 5 RICHIE (coming soon)

And don't miss their follow up HEA's
CADE & ANNA (coming soon)
SIMON & ROSE (coming soon)
STEFAN & EL (coming soon)

CADE

Anna James is single again, finally. In her opinion, men are self-centered and will never love her for who she is, a beautiful, plus-sized woman. All except the fantasy man that she meets in her dreams every night for last five years.

She just never expected her fantasy to be a real live alpha shifter...

Cade Le Beau isn't what he seems. He's a billionaire wolf. A Shifter. He laments his missed chance six months ago to meet his fantasy woman in the flesh. Just as his second chance presents itself, his fantasy woman, his mate, is threatened by the local mob boss and her ex-husband. Now, he has forty-eight hours to deal with this threat once and for all or chance losing her again.

Is it Anna who's in danger, or the humans who unwittingly threaten her?

THOMAS: Le Beau Series

The heat is on the moment they lay eyes on each other. Neither age, children, horrid ex-husbands nor mob bosses will stop this love affair.

SIMON

Four years of honorably serving his country has left Simon, Cade's younger brother, damaged and trapped in wolf form. Little did he know the only person with the ability to heal him completely would be found at home. Literally. Now that he's found her, he is desperate to claim her.

Rose is a beautiful, voluptuous woman with limited experience with men. Although she's confident, she still has reservations. Never having a family of her own, her fear of abandonment has her fleeing romantic relationships and doubting herself.

Travis is insane. A deadly loose cannon that a secret organization hired to destroy the Le Beau family by denying them their mates. Permanently.

Simon's dream will be lost forever unless he is able to maintain human form.

Rose needs unconditional love and a mate to create the family she's always wanted.

Travis's all-consuming drive is to take Rose for himself.

Will Simon ever be whole again, able to claim his mate, giving Rose the love and family she so desperately craves? Or will Travis destroy them both?

STEFAN

V.A. Dold

El is a beautiful, successful, plus-sized woman suffering a debilitating humiliation that has left her hating all handsome, wealthy men exactly like Stefan Le Beau. Unfortunately for Le Beau, she's known him since she was sixteen and was totally snubbed by him. To her, he's a hound dog and a man-whore.

Stefan is a playboy to the extreme with one hard and fast rule: date a woman only once, take her to bed and be gone before morning. Until El.

Stefan's dream of finding his mate comes true when he bids two hundred thousand dollars to win a date with El at Simon's charity ball. Money well spent in his opinion.

Now, if she would only talk to him. Or look at him. Or touch him, or…like him.

Can Stefan convince El he's a reformed man?

Can El learn to trust a man who is the epitome of what she avoids and could shatter her heart?

It will require drastic, strategic measures from the entire family to make this mating happen.

THOMAS

Julia is happy with her place in the shifter community as the owner of the famous shifter bar, The Backwater. But the life she's created for herself isn't enough to satisfy her crazy-ass mother, Lucinda, who shops her and her sister, Krystal, around to the pure blood shifters like pieces of meat. Only a born shifter mate is good enough for her girls.

Thomas James has his hands full as the shifter king's head of security. He certainly wasn't looking for a girlfriend during the first annual shifter gathering. He had the king and queen to protect, not skirts to chase.

THOMAS: Le Beau Series

A childhood of emotional and physical abuse by his birth father has left Thomas emotionally unavailable and uninterested in romantic relationships. His father Tim's cruelty to his mother and brother molded him into an extremely protective person. No one messes with his loved ones without answering to him.

Even though Julia and Thomas are destined to be mates, the obstacles standing between them and their happily-ever-after seem insurmountable.

Lucinda insists Julia stay away from the filthy human.

Tim is trying to kill every one Thomas loves.

The mysterious Benevolent Sovereign, who is trying to overthrow the throne, has sent swampers to attack Thomas and destroy Julia's livelihood.

With family like theirs, who needs enemies?

Will Julia and Thomas's happiness be snuffed out before it has a chance to begin or will they forge through - obstacles be damned.

What is next in the Le Beau series?

V.A. Dold's
Next book:

Richie
Book 5 of the Le Beau Series

**Also watch for the follow-up
Le Beau Series HEA
(Happy Ever After)
Cade & Anna
Simon & Rose
Stefan & El**

Printed in Great Britain
by Amazon.co.uk, Ltd.,
Marston Gate.